TRUE
BETRAYER

Books by Robert Elmer

www.elmerbooks.org

ASTROKIDS

PROMISE OF ZION

ADVENTURES DOWN UNDER

THE YOUNG UNDERGROUND

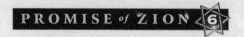
PROMISE *of* ZION 6

TRUE BETRAYER

ROBERT ELMER

BETHANY HOUSE PUBLISHERS
MINNEAPOLIS, MINNESOTA 55438

Published by Bethany House Publishers
A Ministry of Bethany Fellowship International
11400 Hampshire Avenue South
Bloomington, Minnesota 55438
www.bethanyhouse.com

Printed in the United States of America by
Bethany Press International, Bloomington, Minnesota 55438

Library of Congress Cataloging-in-Publication Data

Elmer, Robert.
    True betrayer / by Robert Elmer.
        p.   cm. — (Promise of Zion ; 6)
    Summary: War breaks out following Israel's 1948 declaration of independence,
finding Dov and Emily at Yad Shalom kibbutz helping old friends—and perhaps a
new enemy—prepare for the approach of Arab soldiers, as Dov struggles with
questions about his faith.
    ISBN 0-7642-2314-3
    1. Israel-Arab War, 1948–1949—Juvenile fiction.   2. Palestine—History—
1917–1948—Juvenile fiction.   [1. Israel-Arab War, 1948–1949—Fiction.
2. Palestine—History—1917–1948—Fiction.   3. Jewish Christians—Fiction.
4. Christian life—Fiction.]   I. Title.   II. Series: Elmer, Robert. Promise of Zion ;
6.
    PZ7.E4794Tr 2002
    [Fic]—dc21   2002009663

To Tom and Evelyne Gohlke—

> . . . and let us run with perseverance
> the race marked out for us.
>
> —Hebrews 12:1b

ROBERT ELMER is the author of several other series for young readers, including ADVENTURES DOWN UNDER and THE YOUNG UNDERGROUND. He got his writing start as a newspaper reporter but has written everything from magazine columns to radio and TV commercials. Now he writes full time from his home in rural northwest Washington state, where he lives with his wife, Ronda, and their three busy teenagers.

CONTENTS

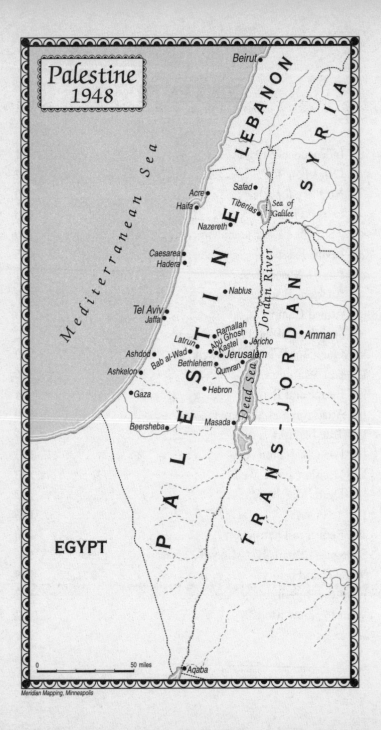

Palestine
1948

Beirut

LEBANON

SYRIA

Mediterranean Sea

Acre
Safad
Haifa
Tiberias
Sea of
Galilee
Nazereth

Caesarea
Hadera

Nablus

Jordan River

Tel Aviv
Jaffa
Ramallah
Abu Ghosh
Amman
Latrun
Kastel
Jericho
Ashdod
Bab al-Wad
Jerusalem
Bethlehem
Ashkelon
Qumran

Gaza
Hebron

PALESTINE

Dead Sea

TRANS-JORDAN

Beersheba
Masada

EGYPT

0   50 miles

Aqaba

Meridian Mapping, Minneapolis

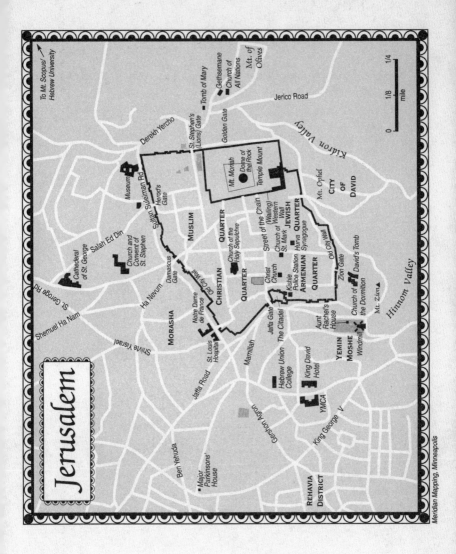

Jerusalem

To Mt. Scopus/
Hebrew University

Tomb of Mary
Gethsemane
Church of
All Nations
Mt. of
Olives

Jerico Road

St. Stephen's
(Lions) Gate

Golden Gate

Derekh Yercho

Kidron Valley

Museum

Herod's
Gate

Sultan Suleiman Rd

MUSLIM

QUARTER

Mt. Moriah

Dome of
the Rock

Temple Mount

Mt. Ophel

CITY
OF
DAVID

Cathedral
of St. George

Salah Ed Din

Church and
Convent of
St. Stephen

Damascus
Gate

Old City Wall

Church of the
Holy Sepulchre

Street of the Chain

(Wailing)
Church of Western
St. Mark   Wall

Hurva

JEWISH
QUARTER

Synagogue

Old City Wall

St. Geroge Rd

Ha Nevim

CHRISTIAN

QUARTER

Christ
Church

Kishle
Police Station

ARMENIAN

QUARTER

Zion Gate

David's Tomb

Shemuel Ha Nam

Notre Dame
de France

MORASHA

Jaffa Gate

The Citadel

Aunt
Rachel's
House

Church of
the Dormition

Mt. Zion

Hinnom Valley

Shivte Yisrael

St. Louis
Hospital

Mamilla

Hebrew Union
College

King David
Hotel

YEMIN
MOSHE

Windmill

Jaffa Road

YMCA

Ben Yehuda

Gershon Agron

King George V

Major
Parkinsons'
House

REHAVIA

DISTRICT

0   1/8   1/4
          mile

Meridian Mapping, Minneapolis

INDEPENDENCE DAY

May 14, 1948

"Turn it up! Turn it up!" Thirteen-year-old Dov Zalinski raised his voice as he looked around the crowd in Anthony and Rachel's tiny living room. He could hardly breathe, much less hear David Ben-Gurion's voice.

"Terribly sorry, it's up as high as it will go." Anthony Parkinson shrugged his shoulders. "Everyone is going to have to be still if we want to hear this."

Anthony might as well have been talking to himself. The neighbors continued to buzz nervously, and Dov fidgeted as he glanced at the Parkinsons' wall clock once more.

Half past four. The announcement had already started. By this time maybe it was over. Hadn't it said in the special edition of the *Jerusalem Post* that the chairman of the Jewish Agency would make an announcement "sometime after four" that afternoon?

"Yeah, it's about time," proclaimed Mr. Zayed, searching for a hair to pull on his bald head. He lived just two doors down, though his Brooklyn accent told them where he had grown up. Most people in Israel had come from somewhere else. "The Brits were here thirty years too long, if you ask me. We're finally on our own. Now if only President Truman would give us a little respect."

That would be the American President Truman, and it didn't surprise Dov that Mr. Zayed would bring up the man's name. Mr. Zayed's neighbor, Mrs. Samuel, on the other hand, didn't seem to concern herself with the departing British troops or the American president. She talked only about her son, Yitzhak, in the *Haganah* army—how she hadn't heard from him in weeks, how he never brushed his teeth, and why wouldn't a good son like him write his own mother a letter once in a while instead of running around the countryside, first out to the Negev, then up to Galilee, risking his life and blowing up who-knows-what. "After all, was that the way he was raised?" she concluded.

Mr. Zayed sighed and shook his head. "The Arabs block our roads, all of Jerusalem can't get food, people are going to starve to death, and you're worried about getting a letter?"

"And why shouldn't I be?" She straightened her back. "Some of us have family, *nu*?"

Without thinking Dov patted his own letter, the one from his mother he carried in his back pocket. It was still there, of course, as it had been for days. He would have been glad if it had been written anywhere in *Eretz Israel,* the land of Israel. That would have been far better, he thought, than having her write from some British military hospital he'd never heard of on an island out in the Mediterranean. He still didn't know how he was going to travel there to see her.

"Whining and complaining," Mr. Zayed went on, raising his voice. "You should be thankful your son has a chance to be a part of history."

"Part of history? *Oy!* I'd be satisfied just to know he was still part of the family." Mrs. Samuel didn't look at anyone as she wore a track in the small living room's round red carpet. Back and forth she went, just like their arguments for the next few minutes.

"Well," Mr. Zayed finally told her, "your getting a letter is the least of our worries."

"How dare you say such a thing?" Her voice raised several notches. "You don't even *have* children, and you pretend to lecture *me*? Why—"

Dov couldn't take it anymore. He poked two fingers in his mouth and blew as hard as he could. Mrs. Samuel nearly jumped out of her scuffed black shoes. Maybe she thought his whistle was another Arab bombshell screaming out of the sky.

"Goodness!" She turned to glare at Dov, clutching her neck.

"Thank you, Dov." Anthony smiled, as if such gatherings happened in his living room every day and their new Jewish homeland declared its independence every Sabbath eve. At last he had their attention, thanks to Dov. He could have whispered and his wife would have heard him out in the kitchen. Anthony turned the volume knob down for a moment.

"As I was saying, I believe we all want to hear what Ben-Gurion has to say. This is an important event."

"Of course we do." Mr. Zayed stared down his beak at the woman next to him. "If Mrs. Samuel would kindly just—"

"Don't you use that tone of voice with *me*!"

"All right, all right!" Anthony held up his hands for silence. "Please. It's nearly a quarter to five."

Dov checked the antique Swiss clock on the wall. It read twenty-three minutes to five.

"What, are we creating a country on a subway schedule?" Mr. Zayed wanted to know. "Back in Brooklyn, we would—"

"There he goes again," interrupted Mrs. Samuel. "It's back in Brooklyn this, back in Brooklyn that. If he had his way, we'd be playing baseball in the streets!"

Anthony cranked up the volume, probably to drown out the bickering neighbors. Dov rolled his eyes and glanced over at his friend Emily Parkinson, Anthony and Rachel's niece. Like him, she was thirteen, though his exact opposite in so many other ways. She'd had life served to her on a china plate, while he'd clawed his way through the worst of Europe's Second World War. At times he doubted she knew there *had* been a war, growing up as she had here in Jerusalem with a silver spoon in her mouth, in a home complete with a driver and a maid.

After the war was over, Dov had worn out a pair of already old shoes traveling to Palestine to look for his family. On the other hand, Emily had probably once had a closet full of fine shoes. Her British army officer father had given her just about anything she'd ever asked for.

Dov could hardly remember his own father. *Abba,* he'd called him when he was little, before Dov had been put into a Polish orphanage for safety, and before the rest of his people were cut off from life in the Warsaw ghetto. And before the slave labor and death camps. He didn't want to think about any of it again. At night, the nightmares still reminded him.

"And now we come to you live from Tel Aviv," the radio crackled, "where the National Council is meeting under extraordinary circumstances."

"I wonder if Daddy is in Tel Aviv." Emily frowned, and Dov knew the feeling. Because, come to think of it, he and Emily Parkinson did have one big thing in common: Both were separated from their parents.

Emily's father was probably still in the country, if it was true he'd been reassigned to help British troops evacuate. Anthony said Major Parkinson had left just before Emily had returned to their old home in Jerusalem looking for him. That meant he was in Tel Aviv, or maybe Haifa. No doubt the major thought his daughter was well on her way home to England, if not already safely there. He would not be pleased about this surprise.

"With the final departure of British forces tonight at midnight," continued the radio announcer, "Mr. David Ben-Gurion and other Yishuv leadership have announced the formation of a new government. . . ."

As far as Dov was concerned, the best part of Emily's story was hearing how she had been stuck on the island of Cyprus after her ship's engines had broken down. She'd kept her promise to Dov to search for his mother and had finally found her on the island, in a refugee holding camp. After all these years, and so close! When she'd told him *that* story, it had been the first time Dov had ever wanted to trade places with a girl.

"A new government," droned the voice, "the first Jewish government in thousands of years."

Dov juggled the announcer's words with his own worries.

If Imma *made it to Cyprus, so can I.*

Of course, it wouldn't be easy. Not now, with the Arab blockade. From what Emily had told him, his mother wasn't well. Not well at all. That was only more reason for Dov to find her as soon as he could.

"History in the making . . ."

Never mind history. Emily had also confirmed that Dov's father had died on Cyprus, if a gravestone was proof. Even his imma didn't know the whole story. Dov's only other family had been his brother, Natan. That was another nightmare. If he closed his eyes—and he didn't dare—he could still see the way Natan had fallen backward from the Old City wall, still hear the sickening sound of the gunshot that had cut down his only brother.

And for what crime?

Another announcer interrupted Dov's thoughts, this one's voice scratchier and more distant, as if he was speaking from across a meeting hall or auditorium. The voice seemed older and more tired, as well. From his spot on the floor behind the coffee table, Emily's Great Dane, Julian, perked up his ears, making him look a little like the RCA record advertisement. In fact, everyone in the Parkinson living room couldn't help but lean toward the radio.

"It's Ben-Gurion!" whispered someone, though they all knew it had to be the Jewish leader.

"By virtue of the national and historical right of the Jewish people and of the resolution of the General Assembly of the United Nations, we hereby proclaim the establishment of the Jewish State in Palestine to be called Israel."

Mr. Zayed grinned and clapped his hands together. Mrs. Samuel glared at him to keep quiet, but then everyone else began cheering and clapping, too. Emily's aunt and uncle hugged. Julian woofed.

Dov looked over at Emily, as if she would know the answer to his question.

"That's it?" he whispered. She nodded. Israel had declared its independence. After too many years, the Jewish people had their nation.

Dov wondered if Ben-Gurion's words would make any difference when he tried to push through the Arab blockade to find his mother. Probably not.

Still, he had to go. Before it was too late.

DANDELION TEA

My dearest Dov,

At first I could not believe it when your friend, the kind Emily Parkinson, said she knew you. After all these years, a miracle! To me, she surely was an angel. . . .

Emily still remembered that part of Mrs. Zalinski's letter to Dov. She'd read it, too, though perhaps not as many times as Dov had. Still, she felt absolutely nothing like an angel as she stood in her aunt and uncle's front doorway the next morning, her knees knocking. Angels, after all, did not shake with fear.

"I'm just telling you, miss. You need to be ready for massive attacks." The young Jewish soldier blocking her way out looked as if he had shopped at a military rummage sale. His dented helmet might have been worn by a British infantryman during the First World War, and his olive green shirt didn't match his khaki shorts. His frowning partner looked equally mismatched. "The Syrians are already attacking from the north. The Egyptians from the south, along the coast, through Gaza. And the Jordanians . . ."

His young voice cracked, and he bit his lip. "If you have anywhere else to go, you should go there now. This is a dangerous spot, right here next to the Hinnom Valley."

"She's with us," said Uncle Anthony from behind her. Emily stepped aside to let him by and saw his arms were full of radio equipment. "Captain Anthony Parkinson. I'm with the Haganah."

The soldiers' eyes widened.

"He's a radio announcer," said one soldier. "I've heard him."

Emily's uncle gave a quick bow.

"At your service, gentlemen."

"I'm sorry, sir, we didn't know." Both young recruits snapped to attention.

"Sorry I can't salute. My hands are a bit full, as you see." Uncle Anthony hefted the box in his arms. "Thanks for the warning, but we're well aware of the danger. Moving the station to a safer place, you see."

Even with Uncle Anthony's Haganah connections made known, Emily couldn't help but squirm at the feeling she was being stared at. Where was Julian when you needed him? The old Great Dane rarely woke up from his long naps to growl at visitors anymore.

"My niece," explained Uncle Anthony, and they nodded. "We'll be quite all right, boys, thank you."

Finally they nodded and backed away. One saluted again and stumbled backward over a loose pavement stone.

"*Shalom,* Captain Perkins," said the first one, shouldering his rifle.

Parkinson, Emily silently corrected him. Her uncle, a *captain*? Everything was changing now. A new country, a new army . . .

The two soldiers were off to the next town house on the block to offer their warnings. Mrs. Levy next door would probably go into a tizzy, along with her yappy dog, Mitzi. The soldiers would soon find that out for themselves.

"They act as if they've never seen a pretty face before," Uncle

Anthony mumbled, then glanced at her. "Were you going some-where?" he asked.

"Just over to Saint Andrew's to check on the girls."

The girls. That would be the dozen orphans Dov had led out of the Jewish Quarter, over the wall, and practically under the noses of the Arab troops that still surrounded the Old City.

"But you're not going there alone, I assume."

"I thought I'd air Julian."

Of course, her main concern was not taking her dog for a walk but rather feeding twelve hungry young girls. With the blockade, that was proving to be a sight more difficult than even rescuing the poor orphans had been.

"I see. Then take Dov with you, as well. I'll be back soon."

The door slammed and Emily turned back toward the kitchen in time to see Dov scouring Aunt Rachel's bare cupboards with his eyes. Julian sat at Dov's feet, his tail thumping the cool tile floor. She tried not to notice the ribs showing through her dog's sides.

"I already checked them this morning." Emily did her best to look cheerful as she walked in. That trick had always worked for her father.

"Smile, princess." That's what he'd always told her when she cried, like the time she lost the silver locket with her grandmother's picture. Or when she skinned her knee walking Julian, the day she was wearing her new pink dress on her ninth birthday.

"Chin up," he would tell her. *"I daresay it's never as bad as it seems."*

This time, though, the tight grip of hunger in the pit of her stomach told Emily that it probably was as bad as it seemed. Of course, she wouldn't dare say so out loud. She hardly dared think it. But for once, Daddy was wrong.

"Uncle Anthony wants you to come with me to Saint Andrew's." She tried not to think of the cracker and small piece of well-aged cheese Aunt Rachel had doled out for breakfast. And she tried not to think of how hungry the little girls had to be, though none of them seemed to complain. Dov nodded without an argument. Perhaps he was just too famished to care.

Neither of them spoke as they hurried along the hillside and up the pathway to the Scottish Presbyterian church and hospice at the top of the hill. Built like a crusader castle, it took the high ground overlooking the Hinnom Valley directly across from the southwest corner of the Old City walls—even higher than the nearby Talbiya neighborhood. From a pole mounted on the highest tower flew a cheery Scottish flag, its white X-shaped cross set on a deep sky-blue background. As they took the two steps up to the front door, Julian hung back, sniffing at a patch of flowers.

"Hello, Mrs. Abernathy?" Emily called between knocks. "Mr. Abernathy?"

Two minutes later a wizened face peeked out at them from behind the tall, arched entry door.

"Ah, so good to see you!" Mr. Earl Abernathy's teeth clicked when he spoke, and his clear blue eyes sparkled a welcome as he pulled open the door. Emily guessed the caretaker and his wife probably didn't see many visitors these days. "The girls have been waiting for you to re—"

"Emily!" A dozen young girls all shouted and giggled and jumped at the same time when Dov and Emily stepped inside. "Emily and Dov and Julian!"

Emily had to laugh at the sight of twelve freshly scrubbed, wide-eyed orphan girls jumping up and down. Kiva and Chava, Frieda and Batya . . . All wore an odd assortment of mismatched charity clothes, rolled up at the sleeves and ankles, all of which smelled of mothballs and soap flakes.

Julian obliged them by sauntering up to wash their faces.

"Did you bring us something to eat, Dov?" asked little Batya. She had always been the first to ask questions, the last to understand. "We're hungry. All we had for breakfast was—"

"Shh!" Frieda Horowitz clapped a hand over the younger girl's mouth. "That's not polite."

Mr. Abernathy smiled sadly and patted Batya on the head. "A nice steaming plate of haggis sounds good to me right now, too."

"Hooray! Haggis!" Batya repeated, then paused to look up with a wrinkled nose. "What's haggis?"

"A pudding boiled in a sheep's stomach," said an older woman, coming down the stairs into the large entry foyer. This part of the church looked like a comfortable hotel and had been built as a guesthouse, a hospice, a piece of the British Isles for weary pilgrims. The entrance to the church sanctuary, which very much resembled that of a proper Scottish *kirk,* angled off outside and to the left of the main entry. "Even though I'm as Scottish as my dear old husband here, if you ask me, haggis is disgusting. Heaven help me for saying that, but it's so."

"Sheep pudding?" Batya repeated, still confused.

"Never you mind, little one." A gold tooth glimmered behind Mrs. Abernathy's smile. "You don't want to know. Good Sabbath, Dov."

"Good Sabbath," replied Dov.

Batya took Mrs. Abernathy's hand as they padded across the tile floor toward the kitchen.

"You'll all join us for a cup of tea," asked Mrs. Abernathy, "won't you?"

"Oh." Dov hesitated. "We were just—"

"Nonsense." She took him by the arm and led him through the tiled foyer to the kitchen. "Everyone could use a little something in their belly. Even if it is just hot water."

Mrs. Abernathy quickly made herself busy boiling tea for sixteen over a tiny kerosene burner. The sickly blue flame fussed and sputtered, and Emily wondered if the woman had enough fuel. Since the blockade had shut down the main highway, everyone in Jerusalem needed kerosene almost as badly as food.

"Tea for everyone!" said Mrs. Abernathy, setting cups in front of each place on the large table. Emily could tell the kindly old woman had cooked for larger crowds than this. But that was during happier times, back when guests from around the world had filled this guesthouse during their visits to the Holy Land. Emily could imagine the travelers that had once come here. She could almost hear them trading stories about their visits to the Sea of Galilee, or their trek to the ruins of Solomon's stables at Megiddo, or to the historic sites in the Old City of Jerusalem. But now the echoes of the girls' voices filled the room.

"With milk and two cubes of sugar?" asked Batya. She sat on two Church of Scotland hymnbooks so her elbows could reach the table.

"Of course!" replied the old woman, chuckling. "Three, if you like! And a big beef bone for Julian!"

Emily and Dov exchanged looks. But the girls gladly played the game, pouring make-believe cream from a cracked, empty pitcher with delicate painted pink flowers. The pretend sugar cubes were dropped in next, after which Batya asked the others if they'd like one or two more.

Plop, plop. Emily took two lumps but couldn't help a quick look at her hostess.

"Oh, it's quite all right," explained Mrs. Abernathy. "A little make-believe never hurt anyone. I would'na want to tease the dog, however. I'm sorry we don't have a proper bone for him. He looks . . . a mite skinny, wouldn't you say?"

Emily nodded quietly. Julian nestled at their feet while Dov scratched his ear. Pretty soon Julian's leg thumped the floor.

"Mrs. Abernathy, do you think they're all right?" Emily couldn't shake the question from her eyes.

"*Ach,* never you worry. You did the right thing, bringing the girls here." Mrs. Abernathy patted Emily's hand. "They could'na done very well in the Old City."

That was true, but Emily wasn't sure they were surviving much better outside the Old City walls, here in the "New" City. At least here they weren't under attack. Not yet.

"Besides," added Mrs. Abernathy, "what were Earl and I going to do in this big building all alone? Would we just lock the doors and go home to Edinburgh?"

"Hear, hear." Mr. Abernathy tapped the end of his spoon on the table in agreement. "It's going to take more than a little war—"

"Earl." Mrs. Abernathy's warning was low but clear.

"Yes, right." Like Emily, he knew what she meant. Don't worry the girls.

"And look at us." The woman spread out her hands. "God has provided all our needs according to His riches in glory by Christ Jesus. Philippians chapter four."

Emily knew Dov might not recognize the New Testament reference. But he couldn't help seeing this old couple's faith. And neither could she.

What did it matter that the lukewarm tea tasted like dandelions? At least it filled their stomachs . . . for a bit. Emily knew, though, that the comfortably full feeling would last only a few minutes. Too soon Batya's stomach would be rumbling again, along with those of the rest of the little girls.

Emily looked around the dining room at the paintings of Scottish hills and castle ruins. In a way it reminded her of another dining room back home.

Home. Where was that exactly? Her home here in Jerusalem

was now only a burned-out shell, the target of a fire bomb set after her parents had left it, only days ago. She imagined the ashes were hardly cool. And England? That was no more a home to her than Timbuktu. For now this cozy dining room in the lovely old Saint Andrew's Hospice, with these people, felt as much like home as anywhere.

"I'm still hungry," said Batya. "Are you sure I can't have some of that sheep pudding?"

"No." Emily looked around the table at the fidgeting girls. Most had finished sipping their drink and were starting to slide off their chairs. "Dov and Julian and I are going to find you something even better to eat than that. Aren't we, Dov?"

"We are?" Dov looked at her with big eyes. Julian wagged his tail weakly at the mention of his name but didn't lift his head.

"We certainly are." This time Emily was sure of it. They would find some food for these kindly Scottish caretakers and for the girls. If they didn't, who would? She shuddered at the thought, and once more her own stomach rumbled.

NO PLACE
FOR A JEW
3

Come on! By Sunday morning Dov decided his own stomach could rumble just as loudly as Emily Parkinson's. His question was, what was taking her so long?

He kicked a stone off the top of the hill and watched it tumble down into Hinnom Valley. Behind him the faint strains of organ music escaped the walls of Saint Andrew's, as they had for the past ten minutes. Weren't the Parkinsons done yet?

"Hey, Dov!" The little voice made him twirl around. But the arched entry of the Scottish guesthouse lay empty.

"Up here!"

Batya waved wildly at him from a second-floor window.

"Oh." Dov jammed his fists in his pockets. "What do you need?"

"Could you bring me a box of sugar cubes when you get us food?"

"Sugar cubes. Right. I'll add it to my list, next to licorice sticks and roast beef. Anything else?"

"Chocolates would be nice."

"Sure thing." He shook his head. "I'll go soon. I'm just waiting for Emily to get out of her . . . service."

Whatever it was had stretched into fifteen minutes, and Dov was ready to leave without them. It wasn't as if it was a *real* Christian service, at least not the way he understood it. Five people in a church that could seat over a hundred? What were they *doing* in there? He looked around to make sure none of the girls were watching, then slowly tiptoed up to the outside church door. What would happen to him if he just peeked inside? Surely God wouldn't get mad at him for that, would He?

He imagined the rabbis back in the Old City wouldn't be too pleased. But really, what could all the fuss be about? And besides, Emily was forever telling him that her Jesus was Jewish. Maybe Dov should find out for himself. He took a deep breath, slowly pulled open the door, and peeked inside.

The thumping of his heart slowed. It was just a foyer. An entry. But now he could hear the music clearly. A wheezing organ pumped out a melody Dov did not recognize, and a few lonely voices joined together in the words to the odd music.

Several more steps brought him around the corner, where he saw row after row of empty wooden pews. The ceiling rose to an impressive height, drawing his view to a wooden cross mounted high on the far wall. Was that it? There were no men in robes, no incense smoke, no graven images or statues. Just Emily, her uncle Anthony and aunt Rachel, and Mr. and Mrs. Abernathy huddled around the organ, singing an "Amen" ending to the music he had heard. Still . . .

This is no place for a Jew, Dov told himself. Yet he lingered for another moment in the shadows, listening to Anthony's voice reading from his Scriptures. The words echoed up to the stone arches, as if a full congregation should hear them. He read about abiding in love, about keeping the Father's commandments.

" 'This is my commandment,' " read Anthony, " 'that ye love one another, as I have loved you.' "

Who could have said such a thing? wondered Dov.

" 'Greater love hath no man than this, that a man lay down his life for his friends. . . . ' "

That was all Dov could take. Besides, what if they saw him? He spun to leave, catching the corner of a small magazine rack and sending it clattering to the floor. But no matter—he was out the doors in a second, bursting into the morning sunshine. He sprinted around the corner before anyone could see him.

Why did I do that? Dov could have kicked himself. He wasn't sure. He caught his breath in the garden, hiding his fears in the heavy scent of hibiscus and honeysuckle. No one would know what he had been thinking; no one would find out. Julian looked up from the hole he had been digging, and Dov whistled softly to him.

"Here, boy."

Julian let Dov scratch him behind the ears, but Dov almost couldn't look into the big, sad eyes.

"I'm sorry." Dov kept scratching, hoping that would soothe the hungry look. "I wish I had a bone for you. Wish I had a bone for *me.*" They sat in the flickering sunshine for a few minutes, quiet. Had the organ music stopped for good? Almost in answer, Emily appeared around the corner a moment later.

"Oh, there you are. We were wondering if you were still waiting."

Dov looked up, as if he hadn't been expecting her. Perhaps she would think he had just stepped outside a moment ago. After all, he might have been in the kitchen, sharing another cup of bitter herb tea with the girls.

"Let's go, you two!" This time it was Anthony, peering around the corner of the building. "The Abernathys think there may be a little kerosene downtown today."

Rachel waved good-bye and went back into Saint Andrews to spend some time with the girls.

Dov lost no time leading the food-hunting expedition down

King George Avenue, looking for any crowds that would signal a food line. But so far the streets were nearly empty. A mixed-breed dog in a doorway showed its teeth at them when Julian trotted by, but the big Great Dane paid no attention, staying at Dov's heels.

"You've got quite the friend there," said Anthony, nodding at the dog. "Whose dog is he now, officially?"

"Hers," said Dov.

"His," said Emily.

They both laughed, but only for a moment. As they walked through the deserted Jerusalem street, the only sound came from the occasional radio. A scratchy Beethoven symphony filtered down from a second-story balcony.

"By the way, Dov," Anthony broke the silence. "If you ever wanted to join us for our Sunday service, you'd be more than welcome."

"Me?" Dov pasted on a confused look. Had they seen him in the back of the church after all?

"Of course you." Anthony nodded. "I just thought perhaps you might like to learn a little something about your Messiah. No pressure."

Dov quickened his step. "I don't think I'll be around much longer."

"Where are you going? With the Arabs blocking the highway—"

"Doesn't matter." Dov decided on the spot. "I'll get out of here somehow. I'll get to the coast if I have to . . . if I have to walk!"

"Oh, Dov." Emily sounded like a schoolteacher. "Surely you don't mean that. You'll just nip up the hills and over to the coast? That's crazy."

"I do, too, mean it." He'd show them. "It's not that far. Only fifty miles to the coast."

"And then what?" she asked.

"Then I'll find a boat or something."

"And go to Cyprus?"

"Why not? You did."

"But that was different. That was before the war started."

"War, no war. Doesn't matter. I'm going to see my mother again."

He didn't add "before she dies." But they knew that was what he meant.

"But, Dov," Anthony broke in. "I told you we'd send a message to her as soon as we could. I know a few people who might be able to help."

"Help with what?" Dov looked him squarely in the eye. "And when? There's no phone, no telegraph, no roads. Besides, I did my part to help the orphans. Now I have to do my part for *me*."

Emily and her uncle exchanged worried looks, but Dov pretended not to notice. He walked a little faster.

Without planning to, they had all three walked in the direction of the upscale Rehavia district, filled with flower-draped sidewalks and stately town houses. Anthony looked at them both with raised eyebrows, his eyes questioning.

"I think we should check the house," answered Dov as they turned the corner to Emily's old street. But with each step closer to the old house, Emily slowed.

"I'm sorry," she whispered, and her voice caught. "But I . . . I just can't."

She shielded her eyes from the sight of the burned-out shell that had once been her home.

Dov thought he understood. He had once seen his Warsaw home in similar condition.

"I should check it out for my brother's sake." Anthony mounted the front steps. "He didn't have much time before he had to leave. Emily, you wait here."

Emily nodded as Dov and Anthony picked their way into the building. Julian bounded ahead with a woof.

"Wait a minute, boy!" Dov tried to follow, but the going was slow. Besides the charred beams that had fallen everywhere, a slippery, sandy soot covered the floor almost ankle deep. He wrinkled his nose at the ruin's acrid, burnt smell.

"Come here, you!" Dov could just imagine Julian covered in soot. He followed the dog into what had once been the kitchen. He could tell by the charred remains of a fine wooden table. Black skeletons of cupboards had dumped piles of darkened cans in a jumble on the floor.

"What's this?" Dov crouched where Julian was excitedly digging, raising a black cloud of dust. "Hold it. Let's look, Julian."

Who could tell what the label had once said? But Dov grinned when he picked up one of the cans and dusted it off. When he shook it, he could hear the promising slosh of something inside. Cooked pears? Or very stewed tomatoes?

"Let's find out."

On the floor he found a table knife, which he used to savagely spear the can from the top. The first try bounced off the top; the second slipped to the side. The third brought a satisfying squirt of sweet, pungent juice, right on his face.

Dov laughed. "Will you look at that!" As Julian woofed, whined, and licked his face, Dov brought the knife down again and again. He hardly noticed the cut to his finger as he pried open a large hole in the top of the can, more than large enough to reach in and retrieve a slice.

"Peaches, boy." Dov popped a slice into his mouth. It tasted tinny and a little strange, he supposed. But he had never tasted better. And then it occurred to him that Anthony and Emily might like to know of his discovery.

"Hey, over here!" he yelled. But when Anthony didn't come right away, he turned aside to find him. A minute later he found Anthony in the basement and led him back.

"I don't know how good the food is," Dov told him, "but it's something. . . ."

His voice trailed off as they entered the kitchen. Julian looked up from the mess on the floor, his mouth sooty black and glistening with peach juice.

"Oh well. I suppose hungry dogs like peaches, too."

But Anthony didn't take it like that. He rushed up to the animal and grabbed the ragged can up with a groan.

"This is not for a dog!" He threw the empty can down, then picked up another. "What have we here, Dov, seventeen or eighteen tins?"

Dov supposed so—minus the one Julian had just wolfed down. Not a bad find, actually—depending on what was inside them. But Dov had never seen such a serious expression on Anthony's face.

"Look, Dov. I've not made any complaint before now. I know Emily has always been rather fond of this beast."

Why is he telling me *this?* wondered Dov.

"But you see what's happening now." Anthony pointed at the dog, who tried to lick his hand.

"He's hungry?"

"Yes. That's exactly the point. The dog is eating food that we can no longer spare."

"But it was just a lousy tin of peaches. I shouldn't have left them."

"Yes, I know that. But it's more than just the peaches."

Dov knelt down and put his arm around the big dog's neck. Julian nearly removed Dov's ear with a peachy slobber-kiss.

"He's a good dog."

"Of *course* he's a good dog. Look, this is as difficult for me as it is for you. But don't you see, Dov? Even good dogs have to eat, and we don't have any food."

Now Dov could tell where this was going. And he didn't like it for a moment.

"All these past weeks, you've said it was all right. You've never minded Julian before."

"Yes, but the shortage has only gotten worse, day after day. The city of Jerusalem is going hungry. *We* are."

Dov tightened his grip on Julian. He couldn't be hearing this.

"Don't tell me you enjoy watching him slowly starve," said Anthony.

"No."

"Even the little food he *does* eat is stolen from us or the mouths of your orphans."

Dov got to his feet, taking Julian's collar. He'd heard enough.

"Dov, don't run away. You know I'm right, don't you?"

Dov didn't answer. He knew. But still he didn't agree.

"Look, there's only one thing to do. Julian's old, besides. It's best for him, and it's our moral obligation."

"No."

"Dov, he needs to be put down."

That was a nice, British way of saying something too terrible for Dov to even think about.

He would not be the one to kill the dog. Not Julian.

Fighting back tears, he pulled on the old dog's collar and ran back out into the street.

ESCAPE PLAN

4

What do we do now? Emily held her head and paced in front of her aunt and uncle's small front window, but the answer was far from her. At least Haganah soldiers had been by again twice since yesterday, filling sandbags and piling them in front of the exposed windows of homes facing the Hinnom Valley on the hillside above. That included their home, of course, though Emily could not say the sandbags made her feel a great deal better. A dark cloud seemed to hang over the little house at 3 Malki Street.

Uncle Anthony and Aunt Rachel sat at the kitchen table, sipping watered-down coffee and talking in the same worried tone they used more and more these days. They almost reminded Emily of her own parents.

"I feel like Joseph's brothers during the famine," announced Uncle Anthony, picking up a small wad of British bills and waving it next to his head. "I've money for food, but there's nothing to buy." Emily knew right away what Bible story he had in mind: the Genesis story of Joseph in Egypt.

"Except your brother isn't waiting for us in Egypt with a big warehouse of grain." Even when things looked glum, Aunt Rachel could still offer them her sweet American smile. "Is he?"

Uncle Anthony chuckled sadly.

"I'm very sorry, Aunt Rachel." Emily didn't know any other way to say it. "But you know we had to share the food we found with the girls."

"Hush, Emily." Her aunt closed her eyes and shook her head slowly. "You don't need to apologize, not for one second. You did the right thing."

"Hear, hear," added Uncle Anthony, holding up the five cans that were left after they had dropped off most of their food at Saint Andrew's. "I happen to love, er, whatever this is. My favorite dish, in fact."

"Oh, go on," Aunt Rachel said. "It's more than we had this morning, isn't it? You stop worrying."

Uncle Anthony raised his hands and looked over at his niece.

"Do I sound to you as if I'm worrying? Tell your aunt I'm not worrying."

Emily had to smile, but he must have seen her staring at the money.

"What's so frustrating," he explained, and the hard edge returned to his voice, "is all this Haganah money left over from the radio station is useless without anywhere to spend it!"

He replaced the wad in an empty sugar bowl on the table, then sighed.

"I'm sorry, Emily. I don't mean to share all our problems with you this way."

"It's all right."

"No, it's not. You needn't worry. We'll get by. God is taking care of us. You know that, don't you?"

"I know that." She really did.

"All right, then." Even without a judge's robe or gavel, Aunt Rachel had her own way of declaring everything all right. "Maybe you should go see where Dov has disappeared to."

That was fine with Emily. She hadn't seen Dov for over an

hour, since he had told them he was taking Julian out "for a moment." But after she slipped quietly out the front door, she soon discovered he had not gone far. Even if she could not see him in the gathering dusk, she could hear him, over behind the climbing pink rosebush that was working hard to take over the corner of the house.

"I'll get you out of here," she heard him promise in between sniffles. She knew better than to stumble upon a boy who was crying. She backed up a couple of steps and started over, shuffling loudly, and heard him catch his breath.

"Dov?" she called. "Are you out here? I think Aunt Rachel is getting supper ready, and—"

"I'm here." Another sniffle, and she could just see him run his sleeve across his nose. "Be there in a minute."

Boys. Always pretending to be tough.

She heard Julian give a soft woof, too, but Dov must have kept a grip on the dog's collar.

"It's all right," she said. "Let him come."

Dov shook his head, which only made her all the more . . . well, perhaps *jealous* wasn't the right word. But she bent down and clapped her hands.

"Here, boy."

"He's fine." Oh, that Dov Zalinski could certainly be a stubborn one when he wanted to be.

"See here, Dov. I know I asked you to take care of my dog for me when I moved away from Jerusalem."

"That's right, you did."

"But you seem to have conveniently forgotten that he was my dog to start with. I grew up with Julian, for heaven's sake!"

"And then you left him."

Emily stepped over and tried to snatch the leash away, but Dov was too quick.

"How dare you!"

"What do you mean, how dare me?"

Emily might have slapped him across his face if Julian hadn't stepped between them.

"I mean," she stuttered, "you needn't be so . . . so . . ."

"So what? You're saying you want him back? Haven't you forgotten something?"

Emily crossed her arms. "And what might that be?"

"You're still leaving as soon as your parents catch up with you. I'm staying right here in Eretz Israel. I'm going to find my mother, and we're going to live here."

Emily started to reply but bit her tongue. As cheeky as Dov could be at times, she could not throw at him the harsh words that now came to her.

After all, she had been the one to see his mother on Cyprus, not quite three weeks ago. She had seen Leah Zalinski weak and dying of tuberculosis. And she knew he would not likely see her again the way he hoped.

Not without a miracle.

"What?" He must have seen her mouth open, then hesitate.

"Nothing." She pressed her lips tightly shut lest a cruel word slip out.

"All right." He gently forced Julian to sit. "Stand back three steps, and I'll do the same."

"What?" Sometimes Emily had no idea how Dov's mind worked. Now was one of those times.

"You watch," he went on. "Don't say anything. Just stand there. And we'll see who Julian likes best."

"Oh." Emily rolled her eyes. "You can't be serious. This is the most stupid—"

"Come on, are you afraid to find out?"

Emily crossed her arms. "I'm telling you, this is absolutely immature."

But she stood there frozen, wondering. What would the foolish charade prove?

"All right, then. I'll do it, if you just answer me one question."

Dov looked at her with his head to the side. "What?"

She paused, but she had to know.

"What were you talking about when I first came out here?"

He didn't answer.

"You were saying something to Julian. I heard you."

Another pause. Finally he shrugged.

"We're leaving."

"What do you mean, leaving?"

"I'm going to the coast. And I'm taking the dog. That way your uncle won't—"

It was Dov's turn to bite his lip, and Emily wondered what he wasn't saying.

"Surely you're not serious. The road is blocked."

He had to know that, of course. What else had been in the news the past week? The British evacuation. The seven surrounding Arab countries lining up to invade. The Declaration. The blocked road that was bringing Jerusalem to its knees. The looming war.

"We're not taking the road," he said, as if that were the most logical answer in the world. "We're walking over the hills. Straight out Jaffa Road to the west end of town, and over the hills."

"What are you, a donkey? You can't do that."

"I can and I will. We're going tonight. And you're not going to stop us."

"But, Dov . . ." This had to be the craziest, most foolhardy plan she'd ever heard, even from Dov. But how *could* she stop the stubborn Jewish boy? He was right that she probably couldn't. Unless . . . she remembered what her uncle had said about Joseph's brothers, and a glimmer of a plan tempted her. Perhaps it would work. Or perhaps it would blow up in her face.

"Weren't you at least going to tell us you were leaving?" she asked.

"Well . . ." Dov started to draw a circle in the dust with his toe. "Actually, I was going to leave you a note. You know, a thank-you note."

A thank-you note, she fumed. *After all this, he was going to disappear in the middle of the night, leaving behind a chicken-hearted thank-you note?*

"What do you have to thank us for?" she asked, but there was no answer. Instead, the front door swung open, and Uncle Anthony leaned out into the gathering darkness.

"Supper in two minutes!" he called, his face framed in a dim but cheery yellow light. "And let me say that you've never tasted olives and evaporated milk as good as this!"

Julian bounded back inside, as if he wanted to be first at the table. The popularity contest was over before it began.

They had no more time for silly contests. From now on, whether they left Jerusalem or stayed, their very lives were at stake.

THROUGH A DARK
JERUSALEM

Dov remembered the lines in his mother's letter about her being proud of him. But she didn't know the truth.

There's nothing to be proud of, he thought as he slipped quietly out of the Parkinsons' home that night. *Every time it gets hard, I run. It's as simple as that. That's how I survive.*

He paused to listen for the even, steady breathing of the others. Good, they were all asleep. But he wondered why Emily hadn't tried to stop him. Not that he'd wanted her to, but he'd halfway expected her to squeal to her uncle. Instead, she'd helped him pack his backpack, adding one of the last of their cans.

Fine. If she didn't care, he didn't, either. He would just take Julian and leave, and they would have two fewer mouths to feed. They should be grateful he was doing them this favor. Besides, no one was going to stop him from finding his mother. Not Emily Parkinson, not her uncle, and not the Arabs.

Still he listened. All quiet.

Nobody cares.

He folded his note and propped it like a tent in the middle of the kitchen table before hitching up his cloth sack over his shoulder and backing toward the door. Maybe he shouldn't have left a note. He didn't write very well, not like Emily.

But it was too late for second thoughts. Slowly he pulled back the latch, swung open the front door, and slipped off into the night. He would simply untie Julian's long leash from the shelter in the side yard where the dog slept, and they'd be gone.

For a moment Emily thought she heard a noise, but her mind would not fully let go of her dreams. Perhaps it, too, was just a dream.

Curious, she thought, groggy and not even half awake. *Was that the front door?*

But sleep tugged her thoughts back under the covers. She sighed and burrowed into her pillow once again, and it felt too cozy to wake. After all, she had been having such a nice dream. One about a huge Easter feast with her parents, where she was too full to move, thank you very much.

Tomorrow morning, she would deal with the waking world. But not before.

The directions weren't hard. Straight on Jaffa Road to the edge of town. The hills began to tumble down from there—some up, but mostly downhill. Straight west and a little south. That would bring him to the coast. Dov could almost see the map in his mind.

Finding his way wasn't going to be the hard part. The hard part was the feeling that every shadow watched him and Julian, that every dark alley or side yard in West Jerusalem hid a pair of eyes. And if he brushed too close to the next row of stone buildings, surely someone or something would leap out, wrestle him to the ground, and hold up his escape. So should he keep close to the middle of the streets, where he could jump out of the way more quickly? Or should he hug the shadows, taking a chance that they would not hug him back?

In the end Julian settled the question for him, dragging him down a narrow alley, then left onto Jaffa Road proper.

"You seem like you know the way," Dov whispered, and the sound of his own voice nearly made him jump. He looked around quickly to make sure no one had heard him, but every window he passed was dark, every storefront shuttered. Only an occasional cat came out to investigate their passing and then quickly changed its mind when it caught sight of the enormous dog.

Rrrr— A dirty calico caught Julian's eye, bringing a rumble from deep in his throat.

Dov patted him on the head. "It's okay, fella," he whispered. "Don't worry about it."

After two hours of walking the dark streets, Dov wondered for the first time how well he and Julian might actually hold up. He couldn't open their two cans of food yet. They'd hardly begun, and already hunger was putting a drag on their pace, like a heavy stone anchor. They paused for a moment, but Dov wouldn't, couldn't close his eyes. Not a minute later, he straightened back up.

"Let's keep going, pal."

Julian looked up at him with his brown eyes, wagged his tail once, and led the way. Ahead lay the bare hills at the edge of the city—hills Dov knew the approaching morning sun would turn golden. As they trudged on, he stole a glance over his shoulder; the sky had gone from ink black to deep blue to lightening cream. Soon the shadows would hide them no longer and he would have to find a place to hide.

Emily tried again to snuggle under the sheets to get comfortable. But her belt buckle jabbed her in the stomach, and she wasn't used to sleeping in her hiking clothes. All she lacked were her leather walking shoes. They were parked on the rug beside her bed, ready to be slipped on.

But when she snapped awake a moment later, she remembered the noise of the front door.

Dov left, didn't he?

She already knew the answer as she hurriedly laced up her shoes and slipped out the bedroom door. How long had he been gone? She hadn't intended to sleep so long. What time was it? Four? Or five, even? She checked the kitchen clock. Five-fifteen. Would she be able to catch up? Noticing the note propped up on the table, she added one of her own.

Went to find Dov. Back soon.

Whether that was true depended on how much of a head start Dov had. She realized too late she must have fallen asleep waiting.

Waiting for Dov Zalinski to run away. How silly of her. But here she was, rushing about, ready to give chase.

He's really going through with it, she told herself, and a stab of doubt made her pause by the front door.

If this is what he wants to do, why would I stand in his way?

Why, indeed? Especially this early in the morning, she wasn't sure she knew. But now it was too late for doubts. And it was too late to do anything except follow Dov Zalinski through the shadowy streets of Jerusalem and into the hills beyond.

"Lord, I'm sorry for what I did," she whispered as she slipped out of the shuttered Yemin Moshe neighborhood, following in what she hoped were Dov's footsteps. "I shouldn't have done it. I should have trusted you. I just couldn't think of any other way to keep him from getting into more trouble."

She hurried her pace, almost jogging along the road that took her west through Jerusalem. A woman in a doorway jumped back as Emily hustled past.

"Good morning," said Emily, but she didn't stop to hear an

answer. She wanted only to catch up to Dov before it was too late.

"This is a good place, don't you think?" Dov crouched down in a low spot between two boulders and pulled Julian in closer. A tough little acacia tree would offer a bit of shade when the sun finally came up. But even more important, it would offer cover.

"We could keep walking, but—"

A round of gunfire echoed over the hills. He knew the way would be scattered with Arab villages, and a Jewish boy with a huge dog might not be greeted with open arms.

Julian licked his nose, and Dov smiled.

"You're right. We'll stay here just awhile, until you're ready to go again. You need to rest. Maybe in a little while . . ."

But Dov could hardly finish the thought. They'd been walking six hours, and he'd been awake all night. Julian didn't seem to mind that Dov laid his head down on the big dog's side and promptly fell asleep.

"Where *are* they?" Emily stumbled, picked herself up, and strained to see the hillside ahead. In the early morning light she could see a rough, winding trail, barely more than a donkey path but still passable. She hoped Dov had come this way.

"Dov?" She cupped her hands and yelled. By this time the shops and apartment buildings of the city were behind her. Who would hear? "Dov!"

Only a mourning dove answered, off to the right, perhaps searching for its mate.

WHO-ahh, ahh, ahh, cried the bird as Emily listened.

Five more minutes, she decided, *then I'll turn around.* What else could she do?

But what was that? She cocked her head and closed her eyes, straining to hear. There it was again: a dog barking.

Not that a bark was so unusual in Jerusalem. But this barking sounded very much like Julian, and it seemed almost certainly to come from the hills up ahead, not the city behind. It blended with the distant sound of bleating sheep, bells, and whistling men. She filled her lungs and was about to shout her dog's name, then thought better of it. Instead, she whistled three times, long and low.

Come on, boy. She whistled once more.

Emily was answered not by a happy bark but by the sharp crack of gunfire—first from behind her in the city, then approaching closer and closer. Did local shepherds carry guns?

Pop-pop-pop-pop!

"Heavens! What's this?" Emily spun around in surprise when shouting and shooting erupted from just over the crown of a hill to her left. The sheep were instantly quiet, and she fell to her knees in the dirt as the shooting seemed to surround her. "Please!"

The faceless attackers obviously paid her no attention, only kept shooting. The ancient rocks around her seemed to come alive as they exploded and shattered. A razor-sharp rock shard grazed her left cheek.

"Oh!" she gasped and clapped a hand to her cheek, but her voice was swallowed in the explosions. She didn't know exactly where the shooting was coming from or where she could hide. As she felt a warm trickle beneath her fingers, she cried out to God and buried her face in the rocky trail. Perhaps she could blend into the rocks.

Just as she did, Emily heard a new sound—the screaming of a motorcar's engine, followed by the wild spinning of tires on the trail behind her and a desperate bleating of a horn, almost right above her head. If she wasn't shot, surely she would be run over as she lay in the middle of the trail.

The horn sounded again.

LEVIN'S RESCUE

"You!" a man bellowed at Emily, but she hardly dared look up. Dust had not yet settled around her head, and shots continued to echo around her. "What are you doing down there? Get in the car!"

Emily would not have guessed she looked so foreign, huddled there on the ground. But if she hadn't, she would have surely been shouted at in Hebrew or Arabic. And it was clear from the man's accent that he spoke the King's English quite passably. She guessed he had to be Jewish, perhaps educated in England. Even so, Emily couldn't make herself get up quickly enough. After all, who was he? And what was he doing on this rugged trail in a . . .

She looked up just as another bullet found its mark, smashing the teardrop-shaped headlight on the low-slung green British MG sports car.

"Hey!" yelled the man. But this time he wasn't yelling at Emily. He wheeled around in his small seat and shook his fist at the hillside. "Do you know how much a vehicle like this costs?"

As if in answer, two more shots rained down on them, one hitting and shredding a spare tire strapped to the rear trunk, the other digging harmlessly into the sandy soil a few yards away.

"Don't you know who I am?" the man yelled out, this time in Arabic. Obviously the attackers did not, and they replied with another shot. Perhaps they hadn't heard him. Perhaps they didn't care about his identity. But by now it was no longer a question of Should I? but only How fast can we get out of here? Without argument Emily hopped onto the car's side running board, grabbing the corner of the wind screen as she did. She had no intention of crossing over to the other side of the car, the side where she could now clearly see the attack had come from.

"Please go!" she urged him, and he obliged. Under the circumstances, he doubtless had no intention of dawdling there, either. Emily wondered that he had stopped for her in the first place. With a roar as the tires spun in the loose dirt and gravel, the green sports car fishtailed down the trail.

"Hang on!" he told her, but Emily needed no such advice. She hung on grimly but efficiently, digging her fingernails into the chrome frame and doing her best not to be ejected into the thorny broom bushes that rudely scraped her back. Hanging on became an exercise in survival when they hit another series of potholes. The driver grinned.

Nothing funny about it. Emily couldn't help noticing the young man's twisted smile beneath a trimmed dark beard. As if being shot at were a funny adventure. She would have turned the other direction, but there was no way to do that and still hang on. He kept up his wild steering, as though in some kind of amusement park ride. For the next several minutes of ruthless bouncing, she had no alternative but to hang on.

Thankfully they ground to a stop five minutes later behind the shelter of a large rock outcropping. Emily wasn't sure that she could have hung on a minute longer. Instead, she slipped backward and tumbled into a shallow gully.

"You do that rather well," remarked the driver. He grinned at her from behind his olive complexion, but he made no move to get out of his idling car or to help her to her feet.

So much for gentlemen.

Emily dusted herself off and flexed her tortured fingers, willing the blood back into them.

"Got a little scratch on your cheek there," he told her, pointing to his own cheek.

She'd completely forgotten. Of course, in all the excitement, it hardly seemed important.

"You needn't concern yourself. It's nothing."

"Whatever you say." He kept an eye on the hills behind them, though Emily didn't see anything. "Would you rather ride in the passenger seat this time?"

Emily paused for a moment to size up the situation. Behind her lay the city and the trigger-happy shepherds—or whoever they were. Ahead lay miles of rugged, rolling Judean hills. She imagined they were still at least forty miles from the sea.

"I can't let you go on alone, miss."

What could she say?

"Well, my parents forbid me to ride in cars with strangers," she blurted out. Given the situation and the surroundings, the excuse seemed rather flimsy.

"So that's why you decided to ride outside the car?"

"That's not it at all." Emily didn't like his tone, nor his sheepish grin. "They only meant that—"

"It was good advice." He interrupted her. "But tell me, miss, what did they say about wandering through hostile territory by yourself? You shouldn't be out here."

Emily blushed. "I know that." She wouldn't be telling this stranger her story.

"Yes, well, I could have told you the Arabs around here shoot first and ask questions later. There's a village just over the hill. You're out for a nice walk, then?"

"Not exactly."

He raised his eyebrows, obviously waiting for an answer . . . that did not come.

"Well, then, perhaps you didn't know the British have all left the country."

He means, what am I doing here.

"I'm sorry to have bent the frame of your wind screen." She changed the subject by pointing to a corner of the windshield where she had been holding on for dear life.

"Not to worry." He shrugged. "The car doesn't belong to me anyway."

Perhaps she should have guessed that by the way they scraped along the bottom of the trail, leaving bits and pieces of exhaust pipe and other scrap metal behind them. This was obviously a one-way trip. But that didn't explain why this man was racing across the hills. Still, Emily didn't care to ask any questions of this odd man, not now. Better not to say anything and just get away, back to Uncle Anthony and Aunt Rachel's house. She began to back away.

"Well?" asked the driver. "Aren't you at least going to thank me for getting you out of trouble back there?"

"Naturally I'm grateful to you," she offered, still inching away. "Mr. . . ."

"Levin. David Levin." He flashed her a bright smile and pressed the gearshift knob forward. "I'd offer you a lift back to the city, but as you can see, I'm in a bit of a hurry."

"Of course." She wasn't sure she would accept the lift anyway. She nodded and waved as he spun away, the small car dragging across a dry creek bed, just down the hill. One of the rear tires looked as if it had flattened, but he bounced on the rim.

Now what? Emily watched until the car disappeared into another gully, and again she wondered how the vehicle had made it this far. She stared for several minutes, unsure what to do next, which direction to turn.

Surely he doesn't expect to make it all the way over the hills in that . . . thing.

Almost in answer to her doubt, Emily heard a distant but wild revving of the engine—as if Levin had taken off or left the ground—followed by the sickening crunch of metal against rock.

Suddenly the hills fell silent.

"Oh dear!" She followed the trail as fast as she could, following the tire tracks down the hill. She didn't have to guess where Mr. David Levin had crashed; she could simply follow the billowy plume of black smoke. And as she drew closer, she could again follow the wild barking of the dog she had heard before.

Both would lead to the same place, she guessed. Except she wasn't at all sure she wanted to see what awaited her.

Dov awoke with a painful start when his head hit the gravel. He sat up and rubbed his eyes as his live pillow raced off.

"Thanks for the warning," he mumbled, scrambling to his feet when he saw how high the sun had already climbed. He'd better be going.

"Come on." He whistled softly to Julian, unsure of who else might be near or how alone he actually was. It seemed quiet enough, except for the dog's eager barks. "Hush, boy. Don't—"

But Julian had his own ideas and headed back up the rise with his nose pressed almost to the ground.

Dov groaned. "You're going the wrong way, Julian." This was no time for the dog to get homesick. He clapped his hands, but the Great Dane didn't notice. "Julian!"

That was as loud as Dov cared to raise his voice. Leaving his pack under the acacia tree, he raced off after the dog. It was four legs to two, he knew—but for once he was hoping that the years would soon catch up with Julian's legs.

"We'll never get there like this." Dov scrambled to keep the dog in his sight. Two miles forward, one mile back. "Come on, Julian!"

As if on a hunt, the old dog continued to howl excitedly. If anyone cared to find him, Dov knew his whereabouts would be no mystery now. Not with all the noise.

But after a few minutes of scrambling after Julian, Dov found they weren't the only ones making noise. Over the next hill—just out of sight, it seemed—he heard shouts.

"Julian!" cried a girl's voice. Surely Emily Parkinson had not followed him this far into the hills? Something stung in his nose just then, and he noticed a cloud of acrid black smoke drifting his way. No matter how odd it seemed, there was no mistaking the eye-watering fumes of burning rubber and gasoline. Now he *had* to see what was going on.

From the top of the next hill he could see it all—a small sports car had rolled to the bottom of a steep ravine, three wheels in the air, the fourth missing. The frame appeared twisted and crushed, and flames leaped out of the top—or rather, what had once been the bottom. Julian was barking at something under the car. The driver?

There was no mistaking who came running from the opposite direction. Perhaps Dov shouldn't have been so surprised. But without stopping to think what could happen next, he rushed down into the ravine, straight toward the flames.

EMILY'S MISTAKE

7

Relief or horror? Emily wasn't sure which to feel. Relief at the sight of Dov and Julian running over the brow of the hill? Or horror at the sight of the awful accident? Without an answer, she ran toward the car, racing Dov to the spot.

"What's going on?" he asked when they were close enough to feel the heat from the flames. "Who do you think this is?"

Emily lifted her hand to shield her face. No time for chat.

"He helped me," she began. "He—"

But her voice caught when she imagined David Levin trapped under the car. It didn't matter now how strange the man had seemed or what he might have done. They had to do *something* to help. Julian, however, had other ideas; he ignored the flaming wreck and barked instead at a pink rockrose bush several paces away.

"Here, help me tip the car over," insisted Emily. Despite the bonfire-sized flames and thick smoke, it was the only thing to do. Dov looked at her for just an instant, his wide eyes a mirror of her own. But he nodded and they both put their shoulders to the side they could reach. She knew if she wasn't careful, her hair might catch on fire. Or the car could simply explode, whether they were careful or not.

"One, two—" Emily grunted as they began to tip the small vehicle.

Still Julian barked, and they heard a moan from behind them.

"What's that?" Dov wanted to know. Emily looked over her shoulder in time to see Julian licking a hand barely visible from behind the rockrose bush.

"Oh no!" she whispered, backing away from her load. Dov stumbled backward when he turned to see the same thing.

"He's over there," Emily cried. She rushed to the bush and fell to her knees, not knowing what they could do or how they could help.

"Mr. Levin!" she gasped. His shirt had ripped, and he looked scraped up from being thrown from his car. But at least he hadn't been trapped underneath.

"Watch out!" shouted Dov, who dove for cover as the car turned into a fireball. Julian scrambled to safety, as well. They grabbed David Levin by the arms and dragged him to safety.

"My arms!" the man moaned without opening his eyes. Emily guessed he might be in shock, so they tried to make him as comfortable as a man could be on a bed of rock. Julian volunteered to lick the man's face, but Emily held him back.

"At least he's not bleeding all over the place," said Dov. "I've seen—"

"You don't need to tell me," Emily cut him off, then nodded at the backpack a few feet away. It must have been launched from the passenger seat. "Get that rucksack for me, will you? Perhaps he has some first-aid supplies."

Dov did as he was told, returning with the pack. He wrinkled his nose at a rolled-up bundle of flowing white Arabic-style clothes. An odd choice of clothing for a Jew, Emily thought, but they could use the cloth for bandages if they needed to. Then Dov pulled out a small supply of dried apricots and pita bread, wrapped in brown paper and carefully tied up with string. That certainly might come in handy for a traveler crossing the mountains. Finally Dov held up a khaki green canvas-covered army surplus canteen like a prize.

"He's prepared, all right," Dov stated. "He has two of these, and they both feel full."

"Good. Let's give him a sip. We need to wake him." Emily tried not to stare at the burning wreck, propping up the man's bruised head while Dov unscrewed the top cap of the stubby tin bottle and slowly tipped the water between Levin's lips. "Easy." Emily imagined a nurse doing the same thing.

Sure enough, David Levin's eyelids fluttered open as he instinctively coughed and took a small sip.

"Thank you," he whispered once he'd begun to catch his breath. He peered at them like a drunkard, first at Emily, then at Dov, then at the canteen.

And that's when his eyes snapped wide to attention, and the injured man popped up like a spring-loaded toy. He gagged and sputtered, spit and sprayed.

"Hey!" Dov defended himself as best he could with his arms. "It's just water, okay?"

"Just water?" Levin grabbed the canteen and took a sniff before answering. They stared at the wild display, and Emily wondered what damage a dazed, half-crazy man could do.

"All right," he finally whispered, settling back down. From calm to maniac, and back again to calm.

"What did you think it was?" Dov wanted to know. "It's your own canteen, isn't it?"

"That's right." The color returned to the man's cheeks. "Of course. I was just, er, confused for a moment. Forget it."

Emily still tried to hold him down, but he relaxed on his own.

"How do you feel, Mr. Levin?" she asked.

"I've had better days." He moaned as he felt his shoulders,

then his arms, then his side. Despite being thrown from the car and rolled into the ditch headfirst, everything seemed unbroken. Remarkable. On the other hand . . .

"Your car's ruined," noted Dov.

"Not to worry." This time Levin waved his hand weakly, but the words were the same as Emily had heard earlier. "The car doesn't—"

"It doesn't belong to you anyway," Emily finished for him. "You've said that before. But, Mr. Levin, are you able to stand?"

"Let's see."

With help from both sides, he managed to rise—slowly—but a moment later grimaced and bent to grip his leg.

"You hurt your foot," said Dov.

"No, the foot is fine. It's the knee that's twisted or something. I've hurt it before, in . . ." His voice trailed off, as if by telling them about an old injury he would spill some kind of secret.

"In . . . ?" Dov was the curious one.

"Don't worry about it, kid. Just hand me my bag and let's go. I'm going to need to lean on your shoulder once in a while."

So they would now be traveling together? To where? Without waiting for an answer, David Levin found a stick to use as a makeshift cane. Next he hitched up his little load and hobbled on down the hill. Even with his limping, though, they would have a hard time keeping up. Again remarkable.

So much for being in shock. Emily shook her head in wonder. She still wasn't sure how someone could simply get up and walk away from such a horrific accident. It made no sense, no sense at all.

She did not follow.

"You go on ahead," she announced. "I need to go home."

"Not that I care," Levin yelled back without turning around. "But our friends have probably seen the smoke by now."

"Who *is* he?" Dov whispered at Emily.

"All I know is that he says his name is David Levin. He won't quite admit it, but I think he might have stolen that roadster. And—"

"And what *friends* is he talking about?"

"Some people shot at us back there." Emily guessed from Dov's question that he'd not met the same problem.

"I'm telling you," Levin tossed a warning over his shoulder the way someone else might toss a peanut shell. "I wouldn't stay here much longer if I were you."

Our friends back there. In all the excitement Emily had nearly forgotten about the ambush and the men in the hills behind them. A distant pop reminded her that David Levin was probably right. Suddenly the prospect of turning around and going home alone didn't sound so good anymore.

"What were you doing following me, anyway?" asked Dov, hitching up his own reclaimed backpack. "Julian and I were going to make it to the coast just fine."

"Is that where you're going?" David Levin had very good hearing, very big ears, or both.

"Tel Aviv," Dov answered. "Or Haifa."

"I like someone who's sure of what he wants. Either way, that's a long hike. Know anyone on the way?"

"No-be," they answered together—Emily's "no" and Dov's "maybe."

"I see."

"We did know some people at a kibbutz," offered Dov. "I was thinking I might stay there on the way across."

"Really?" This time David Levin seemed interested as he looked back at them. "Which one?"

They both paused a moment and looked at each other, as if to see who would answer first.

Emily shrugged. What secrets did *they* know?

"Yad Shalom," she finally answered. "We don't really *know* the people there well, we just stayed there a few days."

"Yad Shalom," Levin repeated. "Thirty-five miles north of the border. The peace kibbutz. Perfect."

Emily thought it odd that David Levin knew exactly where the farm was on the map. And *peace kibbutz,* indeed. Perfect for *what,* he didn't say.

"You can get us in there?" he asked.

"I suppose," answered Dov. "And they have food. I remember lots of chickens. Plenty of eggs."

"Which is more than we can say for Jerusalem," answered the man. "Too bad you can't bring some back with you."

Emily hadn't thought of it that way. But David Levin's words made sense to her, though it would be a desperate move. If they *did* make it to Kibbutz Yad Shalom, what would keep her from returning home with food? Doing that might bring some good out of this insane hike.

Perhaps . . .

As she thought of how they might explain everything to Aunt Rachel and Uncle Anthony, she almost didn't notice that Dov had stopped in the trail right ahead of her. He had peeled off a light jacket and loosened his pack.

"Oh!" She stopped short, stepping on the back of his shoe. "Sorry."

Dov didn't seem to notice her. He was too busy looking at something he'd discovered inside his pack. "What in the world?"

He lowered his voice and pulled out a wad of bills. The look on his face left no doubt it was the first time he had seen them. It might as well have started to snow, right there in the desert in the middle of May.

"What in the world?" he repeated. Obviously their new guide had nothing to do with the mysterious stash. In fact, Emily walked around and blocked the way so David Levin could not see what

Dov had discovered. This was definitely *not* going the way she had planned it.

"I'm sorry, Dov." It was a secret she could no longer keep. "I didn't mean to . . . That is, I only meant to . . ." Her voice trailed off. How could she explain this turn of events?

ATTACK AT
BEIT JIZ

8

"Wait a minute—you?" Dov's face clouded over with a sudden black thundercloud of understanding. "You put this in here? Why?"

By now it was sorely obvious her plan had gone horribly wrong. Though at the time it had seemed the only thing to do, now Emily trembled at what she had to confess.

"Dov, you must understand. You wouldn't let anyone talk you into staying in Jerusalem."

"What does that have to do with anything?" he growled.

"Well, would you?"

"Of course not."

"See? I thought that putting money in your rucksack was the only way to keep you from making a big mistake."

"Oh, thanks, Mother Emily."

Pack still in hand, Dov shoved her aside and followed David Levin.

Emily tried to keep up. "Dov," she said, keeping her voice low. "Don't you see why I did it? Unless I did something drastic, you would have—"

"I would have left?" he asked. "That's my mistake? Going to be with my mother?"

Emily nodded, tears in her eyes. She swallowed hard. "You see, I thought you would discover it before too long, and then you would turn around to give it back."

"Brilliant. Just brilliant."

But Emily still had more to say. And now would be easier than later.

"I'm very sorry, Dov. It was a bad plan. I didn't mean to make you look bad. I was . . . I was wrong. I honestly didn't mean for it to turn out this way."

This time it was Dov's turn to be silent as they picked their way down the trail. David Levin was thankfully out of earshot, a hundred yards ahead.

"You didn't mean for us both to be stuck on this hike, eh?"

Partly true. Dov went on.

"And what if I had just walked away with all the money?"

"I really didn't think you would do that. You're not a thief, Dov. And I know you don't want anyone to think you are."

"Am I supposed to thank you for that vote of confidence?"

"No. I'm just hoping you'll forgive me, that's all."

At that he stopped and turned to face her. He dug the bills out of his pocket and tossed them at her, underhand.

"I don't know why I'm not really angry. I should be. Tell me one thing, though."

Emily lifted her eyebrows.

"What gave you such a dumb idea?"

"Oh." Emily looked down. "You don't want to know."

"Try me."

Emily sighed. "The Old Testament story of Joseph and his brothers."

"Hmm."

Emily wasn't sure Dov knew the story of how Joseph had

hidden a silver cup in his younger brother Benjamin's sack as the brothers were leaving the Egyptian court. It had been a trick designed to bring them back together. Now she almost wished she'd never heard the story. If only she hadn't—

"Ouch!" Emily gave up her "if onlys" when a small rock hit her square on the leg. She hopped on one foot for a moment and looked up to see David Levin staring at them with a fierce expression. With a finger on his lips, he commanded them to be still. He motioned for them to come closer with his other hand. He'd abandoned his cane.

"Hurry up!" He mouthed the words and they crept forward.

"What is i—" Dov started to ask, but David Levin grabbed him by the shirt collar and held a finger to his lips.

"I told you to be quiet!" he hissed. When he pointed through the trees up ahead, they saw why.

"Do they have guns?" whispered Emily. She crouched behind a gnarled pine tree trunk while Dov gripped Julian by the collar. Emily stroked her Great Dane, hoping he would not choose this time to go chasing imaginary rabbits.

"I don't think they do." Levin squinted. Emily herself could make out only three men walking through a distant grove of olive trees on the far side of a small valley. The orchard had been planted in neat rows by some long-ago farmer, and the trees looked quite old, almost wild. The men in traditional Arab dress blended in well.

"They must be from Beit Jiz," Levin explained. "That's the Arab village just over the hill."

The men obviously were in no hurry as they strolled through the orchard. Once in a while one of them would pause to check the trees, perhaps reaching up and taking a branch for inspection. Perhaps they were telling each other the crop would be better this year. Emily thought she could see the glimmer of sunlight on a blade as one of the men split open a sample piece of fruit.

"We're not walking down there," Dov whispered the obvious. They'd have to walk *around* the tiny town, out of sight and well away from the men in the olive grove. That meant scrambling over a large rock outcropping, up and over another hill, and through yet another ravine. Emily sighed. They'd already seen more than their share of such landscape.

"Right," agreed Levin. "Let's be on our way, then."

Emily straightened up and began to look around for an easy detour, but by that time Julian had caught sight of the Arabs in the orchard. Dov just managed to muzzle the dog's mighty woof of greeting.

But that gave Julian the moment of freedom he must have been waiting for. With a mighty shake he pulled his big head free and bounded down the slope to say hello. This was an old dog?

"Julian!" whispered Emily.

"Oh no!" Dov groaned. "Julian, come back!"

David Levin managed to snag one of Dov's belt loops before the boy could give chase, and for a minute Dov looked like a human yo-yo.

"Let me go!" he demanded, but Levin held on.

Meanwhile, Julian bounded down the hillside, woofing at his new friends with the excitement of a puppy. The three men, on the other hand, obviously had a considerably different opinion of Julian. Perhaps they'd never seen a Great Dane before, a dog that easily outweighed any one of them. Or perhaps they would rather have greeted a lion or a wolf than this frightening creature.

Emily wanted to hide her face rather than see what happened next. One of the men pointed excitedly at the incoming freight train on four legs. This got the other two into formation, all waving their hands. The bravest of the three took a few steps forward, shouting and stamping his feet in the dirt, bullfighter style. But Julian didn't slow a step. And the men must have changed their minds in a hurry, turning back toward Beit Jiz and running back over the hill.

"What is *wrong* with that animal?" groaned Levin, rising to his feet. "He's going to get us all killed."

"There is nothing wrong with him," countered Dov. "He chased away the men, didn't you see?"

"Nothing wrong with him at all," added Emily for good measure. But what would happen now?

"Oh yes, he chased them away, all right. They'll just come back with their guns now."

Dov whistled, bringing Julian up short of the hill. Their dog looked back, his big pink tongue flapping wildly, as if wondering why they didn't join in the chase. Or perhaps he had run out of wind by that time. Dov took a step to follow Julian, but David Levin grabbed him again. This time Dov struggled until he was wrestled to the ground.

"Now, you listen to me." Levin rolled Dov over onto his back and planted a finger in Dov's face. "We're going on, but that dog's staying here. Do you understand?"

"You leave him alone." Before she knew what she was doing, Emily had grabbed the back of the man's shirt collar and pulled. It came apart with a loud rip.

"Aargh!" David Levin twisted around and stood up just as Julian came bounding back to join the fight. The dog planted his two large paws squarely on David Levin's chest, sending him tumbling backward. Like a cat, the man rolled away from the huge dog's kisses and got to his knees. Just as quickly, he reached into his pack and produced a small pistol.

"No!" cried Dov. He wrapped his arms around Julian's neck and held on.

"Get out of the way!" ordered Levin. "I'm going to take care of this problem once and for all."

But Emily stepped in front of him, too.

"No, you're not." She stared at him, trying to keep her voice from trembling. "You don't want the people in Beit Jiz to hear us, do you?"

For a long moment he stared first at Emily, then at Dov and the dog. Julian seemed content to sit and catch his breath. Finally Levin mumbled something, lowered his pistol, and replaced it in the pack. In the scuffle his canteens and food had been spread out at their feet. Emily bent to pick up one of the water jugs.

"Don't touch that!" He grabbed it from her and stuffed his things back into the pack himself.

"I was just trying to help."

"Then help me by taking this other canteen. Here. Thirsty?"

Actually, she was. She accepted the canteen from him, the one he had been drinking from before. The first canteen still felt full to the brim.

"Keep it," he told her. Was this his way of trying to smooth things over?

Emily held back as he rose to his feet once more, perhaps too quickly. For a moment he closed his eyes and held his forehead in pain. Dov looked as if he might still want to tackle him, but Emily held up her hand.

"Your head?" Emily had no idea how she could make the switch from attacker to nurse's aide. Dov got to his feet and dusted off while David Levin slowly opened his eyes.

"We've got to keep going, and quickly." His voice was quieter this time, steadier.

"You're hurt," Emily told him.

"Here, give me your arm."

Emily hesitated.

"I said—"

"We're not going without Julian," interrupted Dov.

"All right, fine," Levin gave in. "But if he ever does something stupid like this again, I'll . . . I'll . . ."

Julian licked the man's hand, who only pulled back as if he'd been bitten.

"I don't know *why* I brought you two along."

"Because you need us to help you," replied Emily. "You're not well."

"Hmph. Just remember you can't get over these hills without my help, either."

Emily didn't answer; she knew he was probably right.

"I thought you said he was an old dog who could hardly walk," Levin mumbled.

"Kind of like you, Mr. Levin," Emily replied. "But Julian still has his moments."

Dov kept his own pace next to the dog, his jaw set and his fists clenched. Emily wondered what he was thinking, or what he might do, given the chance. At least she could be thankful that his disappointment in her had been forgotten in his anger at David Levin.

ARMED CAMP

9

"There it is!" Emily pointed up ahead at the low coastal hills—their last climb before reaching the sea. Or was it? Maybe they would never reach the coast and just keep walking, miserable day after miserable day. Had it been a week yet? A month? Not quite; it was only Thursday. After three long days of walking, the time almost didn't make any difference. At least not to Dov.

After all, Day Three of the Great Hike hadn't turned out much better than Day Two, which certainly wasn't any better than Day One. David Levin had grumbled about the dog, but they'd kept on walking. He grumbled about not having the MG to drive, but they'd kept walking. And he grumbled about his traveling companions, but always they kept walking.

Dov, on the other hand, had decided on a better plan: denial. He pretended none of it was real. His stomach had long since given up rumbling, even when he thought about food. He was past being hungry. His lips were cracked, even when he took a sip of water from David Levin's canteen. No problem. Who needed lips, anyway? And his sock was worn through where the hole in his shoe had been growing larger and larger. Maybe he should have ridden Julian. Come to think of it, maybe that wasn't such a bad idea. He just wasn't sure the dog could handle it, or he might have tried.

Even his legs didn't feel as if they belonged to him anymore, and his blistered feet were almost unrecognizable. What would come next after pain and soreness and stiffness? Was there any uncomfortable feeling left to experience?

Dov shuffled along the rocky trail, dragging his toes, kicking up dust, and falling behind the others more and more. Julian plodded along up ahead, though he checked over his shoulder every few minutes.

"Don't forget me and the dog, God," Dov mumbled. He wasn't sure if that counted as a prayer. More like a comment God was welcome to listen to. Whatever happened, Dov would keep walking, as long as it took. He would even leave Eretz Israel for Cyprus, if that's what it took to be with his mother.

But he would reach her on his own power—whatever was left of it. At the moment that didn't seem like much at all.

"Yes, I see it." David Levin quickened his step and waved the map in his hand. "That is definitely your kibbutz up ahead."

"Too bad they don't know we're coming," Dov mumbled. "They could have fixed us a nice hot dinner. Maybe some roast chicken with gravy. Boiled eggs. A big plate of steaming potatoes, doused with butter. Three potatoes. One more? Oh, no thank you, I really couldn't. Well, if you insist. I don't want to be rude. . . ."

He closed his eyes, imagining the feast, going over the menu once more, just to be sure he hadn't left anything out.

"And for dessert, I'm thinking a nice big slice of apple strudel, still warm from the oven, sprinkled with brown sugar, and maybe a tall glass of cold sweetened buttermilk to drink. Oh yes. That would be perfect."

By that time Emily had come back to grab his arm. Maybe the dreaming had taken all his energy and made his legs stop moving.

"What are you doing back here?" she wanted to know. "You look as if you're sleeping standing up."

"Not sleeping. Just—"

"You can save your dreaming for later. You're going to sleep in a real bed tonight. Or at least a real cot."

"That would be terrific." He started to think whether the kibbutz gravy would be dark or light while Emily pulled him by the arm to help him get his legs moving again.

She was right. Unless they had gone terribly wrong, they were finally close to Kibbutz Yad Shalom. They'd left the woods behind sometime earlier that day. Up ahead, Dov imagined the faint scent of the ocean, straight west.

Just the thought of the ocean helped him keep up with Emily and Julian on the downhill trail. The half moon had risen in the east, back over his shoulder, casting an eerie blue light on the rolling, sandy hills. And then Dov blinked at the twinkling of a yellow light, just ahead and over the next ridge.

A star? Not unless stars could play accordion music, clap, and sing folk songs. In spite of himself, Dov moved his legs faster and faster, almost in time to the distant music.

"Come along!" Emily urged him. Dov felt like he was ninety years old, with legs that would no longer move at his command.

"You're not bad with directions," grunted David Levin as he folded his map and stuffed it back into his backpack for the last time. "We're spot on."

"My father taught me," replied Emily. Dov couldn't be sure, but it looked as if her eyes were watering. Why she would cry about arriving at the kibbutz, he wasn't sure. With each step the singing and clapping grew louder, until they could hear the Yiddish words clearly.

"Un mir zainen ale brider," they sang, "We are all brothers. . . ."

David Levin's lips moved, but he said nothing until someone

shouted at them, and they stood frozen and blinded in a beam of light.

Dov blinked and held a hand in front of his face. His eyes hurt.

"Stop where you are!"

They obeyed—especially when they heard the distinct loud *click* of ammunition loading into a rifle. Emily, though, cupped her hands and yelled at the light. Dov guessed it came from a searchlight mounted on the railing of the Yad Shalom guardhouse. Funny, he thought, that the first thing they encountered when they arrived at a farm called Monument to Peace was a guardhouse with a searchlight and a rifle.

"It's just Emily," she shouted. "Emily Parkinson. Remember me?"

The light did not reply, but the accordion stopped playing.

Emily tried again. "We stayed here a few months ago, Dov Zalinski and I. We're friends of Henrik Melchior."

At that they heard some shuffling and murmuring, someone yelling, "Go get Henrik!"

"How about turning off the bright light?" asked David Levin.

Within a few moments Dov heard a whoop and someone running their way. A gate in the wire fence flew open, and a tall young man sprinted up to them with his arms open.

"I knew you'd come back!" It was Henrik, of course. The Danish Jew who had first welcomed them to this place months ago. He wrapped his powerful arms around Dov and hugged the breath out of him. "*Velkommen, velkommen* . . . I mean, welcome!"

Henrik held Dov by the shoulders. He stood perhaps a head taller than Dov and was three or four years older. Still, he looked as if he had rediscovered his best friend.

"How did you know I would come back?" Dov asked. He couldn't help grinning on one side of his mouth. He'd almost forgotten, but Henrik's smile was like that, as infectious as a case of flu after someone sneezes in your face.

"You said you would come back, right?" Henrik shrugged, his own grin large on his face. "I figured you're somebody who keeps his promises."

Am I? Dov shook his head in wonder. He had hardly remembered saying the words. But Henrik hadn't forgotten.

Not to be outdone, Julian woofed his own happy welcome.

"I see you've brought the whole family." Henrik led them inside the gate after they were introduced.

"It's a long story," admitted Emily, and Henrik seemed to know just what she meant.

"I'm sure you'll have lots of stories to tell," he said. "But again, welcome!"

They would hear that word over and over again as they entered the farm. "Welcome back!" and "Welcome to Yad Shalom!" Everyone they met wore the word in their smiles. But even Dov, barely able to keep his eyes open, could see the tight, serious looks behind those smiles. Things were not the same as they once had been at the kibbutz.

"I apologize for all the sandbags and barbed wire," said Henrik's stepfather, Matthias Karlsson, after they had been reintroduced and given a meal of thick, steaming lentil soup and crusty bread, topped off with fresh whole milk to drink. "God brings you back here at a very interesting time."

Interesting time, indeed. Everyone on the kibbutz seemed to be digging trenches or stringing barbed wire or filling sandbags. Even in the dark, people scurried about like squirrels before winter. The singing and clapping started again, like a marching band keeping time.

Dov wasn't sure if he would call the threat of invading Egyptian troops interesting. And he hadn't exactly thought of God bringing them there. Even so, it was hard to disagree with the big dark-haired man in glasses.

"It's not the way we prefer to live here at the kibbutz," continued Matthias in his Scandinavian accent, "but we tell ourselves it's just for the time being."

"Quite all right," put in Emily. "We hadn't expected any grand welcome."

At that Henrik laughed out loud, but he instantly clapped a hand over his mouth, like someone who was trying without success to hold back a cough.

"I'm terribly sorry," he explained. "It's just that last time you were here, well, I would have expected you to say something else, that's all."

"Oh." Emily went on to explain what had happened to her parents, how she had unexpectedly returned to Israel, and why they had come to the kibbutz. Or rather, why *she* had come.

"We were just hoping to buy some food," she added, "and then return as soon as we could to Jerusalem."

Speak for yourself. Dov started to say something, then changed his mind. He didn't have to announce his plans to everyone. So what if they thought he was traveling with Emily Parkinson? It didn't matter anyway. He would just get some food in his stomach, rest his feet a bit, and then he'd be off again.

"Wonderful!" Matthias stroked his dark beard. "And food we have! Plenty of eggs, vegetables . . . It's just that with all this talk of war, the roads have been, well, not so good. I'm so pleased that you made it here safely. But then again, why should I be surprised?"

Dov could think of plenty of reasons to be surprised. Had anyone else made it out of Jerusalem alive recently or found a way across the mountains?

"We have money to buy." Emily patted a bulging pocket in the oversized work pants she wore. "They don't know about this yet, but I think my uncle and aunt would be pleased to spend it on food."

"What about that other fellow?" asked Henrik. He looked around the room. Over in the corner, Julian lapped up his third bowl of water. "Is he going back with you, too?"

"I doubt it." Emily shook her head.

"He didn't really say much about his plans," added Dov.

"David Levin." Matthias nodded in a way that told them the two men were not strangers. Dov could not read if that was a good or a bad thing. And although no one asked, "Do you know him?" Matthias answered.

"We met," he replied, "when I was working with the refugees." That was all, and he cleared his throat to change the subject. "But come along. We have a lot to do before the war starts. And, Dov, I have something that belongs to you."

SNAPSHOTS OF THE
PROMISED LAND

Dov stared at the photos on the wall of the small work building. He gazed at photos of a distant Mount Carmel covered in wispy gray clouds, a seabird against a bright sky, a group of refugees huddled on the deck of the rusty old freighter, fighting the wind. All were reminders of the long voyage that had first brought Dov and so many others to the Promised Land. The photos were almost like dreams he had once dreamed, snapshots of forgotten memories. After all, he had taken them.

"Remember those?" Matthias looked up at the wall above his crooked metal desk and waited for an answer.

Yes, Dov remembered them. It seemed like a lifetime ago, but he remembered every moment of the journey over the Alps, through the Mediterranean, the final wild swim from the freighter to the beach near Tel Aviv, when Emily had practically dragged him out of the surf and saved him. He nodded.

"I hope you don't mind I had the film in your camera developed." Matthias pulled off his glasses and leaned closer for a better look. "But after you left your camera and things on the ship, what else could I do?"

"Especially after I told him I'd met you," added Henrik with his trademark smile. "It was my idea to develop the film. I like the one with the young girls, there, on deck."

"*Ja,* you're a pretty good photographer, Dov, I'd say." Matthias opened a desk drawer and pulled out a small canvas sack. Dirty and ripped along one seam, it looked as if it had been dragged halfway across the continent.

Actually, it had.

"My bag." Dov caught his breath.

"That's right." Matthias nodded. "Your camera, the bank with all those coins in it . . . all there."

Dov hadn't forgotten the bank, either. But he'd never dreamed of seeing it again. Never in a million years.

"Go ahead." This time Henrik picked up the bag and placed it in Dov's hands. "Take it. It's yours."

Of course Henrik and the others didn't know the whole story, and that was a good thing. They didn't know how the money had been collected penny by penny at the Displaced Persons Camp in Germany just after the war. They didn't know all the small sacrifices that had been placed in that blue coin box, just to help the Jews in Palestine. And they couldn't know how each small coin represented the hopes of another Jew who had so wanted to come to Eretz Israel but never would.

Most of all, they could never hear how each coin screamed out Dov's guilt. Or how much of a thief he had been to take that money in the first place, when he had left Europe on his way to Israel.

Thief!

Dov held his palms to his ears, afraid of hearing the accuser once more. For months and months he had outrun it, ever since he had escaped the camp with the money and come to Israel. Only now the voice seemed to face him with new strength.

You're a thief!

"Are you all right?" Henrik wanted to know.

Did he know where the money had come from? If he did, he didn't let on.

"Fine." Dov put his hands down. "I'm fine."

A thief . . . and a liar!

"I mean . . ." Dov took a deep breath and stumbled over his next words. They startled him as much as they did everyone else. "I mean, no. This money isn't mine, you see. It belongs to . . . a collection for Eretz Israel. For the people here."

Dov handed the collection box back to Henrik's stepfather.

"Here, please take it. I can't keep it."

Dov could have whooped when Matthias nodded and took the box. Did the man understand?

"I'll make sure the money gets to someone who can use it." He smiled and winked. He did understand. "But the camera is yours, isn't it?"

"It is," Dov barely whispered. He picked up the old German camera and turned it around in his hands again.

"Don't open the back, by the way," Henrik warned him. "We put fresh film in."

"Fresh?" At first Dov didn't understand.

"New film," Henrik explained. "You know, so you can take more snapshots. Maybe you can take some of us outside when the sun comes out again."

"Sure." Dov nodded, and then he looked around, surprised at the quiet.

The accusing voice was gone.

"Look this way," Dov called to the crew in the trench. Emily paused only a moment from digging, long enough to raise her eyebrows at him. "Okay, bad idea. Just a second."

The trench diggers gave him a moment to line up his camera

and click the shutter, but only once before they returned to their work. They did not, however, smile. And so it had been all over the camp. Some had been working all night; others were just trudging outside for the after-breakfast shift. Next to Henrik, Emily shoveled sandy, rocky dirt out of trenches. Julian did his best to dig his own holes, too.

"I should be getting along to Tel Aviv," Dov announced, rocking back on his heels. Emily didn't look up or answer except with a grunt as she hefted another shovelful of dirt to the far side of the trench. Their mound was growing higher by the minute.

"You needn't apologize," she told him. "Just do what you must."

"What about the food you were going to bring back?" Dov tried to think of something else to say. Anything to stall, to keep from walking alone down the dusty road that wound out to the main highway.

"My mother . . ." Henrik teetered with his own shovelful of dirt before he tossed it out of the waist-high ditch. "She's getting some things together, loading them onto Lizzi and Laslo for you."

Lizzi and Laslo. Dov's blank look asked the question for him, and Henrik was ready with one of his signature smiles. Even up to his waist in a ditch and covered with dirt, he smiled. What was wrong with him?

"Our two donkeys. You'd be surprised how much they can carry." Henrik turned to Emily with a friendly warning finger. "But they're just on loan, remember. We're going to need them back as soon as you can get them to us."

Emily nodded. "I don't think we'll have anywhere to keep them in Jerusalem. We'll get them back to you as soon as we can."

"We?" Dov wondered what she was thinking. But he was not willing to be volunteered for the trip back east over the hills, back up to Jerusalem. Not this time.

"Like I said . . ." he began once more, but Emily and Henrik had turned back to their shovels again. If Dov hadn't known better, he might have thought it was a game, the way they paced each other and the dirt again began to fly about their heads. First Henrik, then Emily, then Henrik, then . . . Emily's spade clanked.

"You hit a rock," Dov told her.

"Mmm-hm." She leaned into her task, but the rock obviously would not budge. Her face turned red, and beads of sweat had set up about her forehead.

"Here, let me try." Before Dov really knew what he was doing, he had set aside his camera and hopped down into the ditch. He grabbed a shovel and pointed the blade into the loose ground on the other side of the small boulder.

"There you go." Henrik sounded like a football coach. "Now both of you lean into it. One, two . . ."

With two shovels Emily's boulder finally began to break the surface, a shy whale coming up for air for the first time.

"Almost!" Dov gritted his teeth and leaned. Finally the rock breached and rolled over. Dov caught himself grinning.

"Good job, you guys," said Henrik. "You work together pretty well."

"No, we don't." Dov knew better. "She's always bossing."

"And he's perpetually complaining."

Dov wondered why she didn't say *always* instead of *perpetually*. But they both kept shoveling, faster and faster. And now the three shovels made an even bigger cloud of dirt: Henrik, then Dov, then Emily.

"You really think . . . this is going to stop . . . the Egyptians?" Dov asked between shovelfuls.

"No." Henrik shook his head. "It won't stop them. But the Haganah has only asked us to slow them down. What else can we do? God is in control."

If this is God in control . . . Dov looked around at the teams of people still rolling out more barbed wire. Behind them, a couple of men were positioning an old cannon behind a protecting mound of dirt. It looked like some kind of rusted antique, perhaps from the First World War, perhaps older.

"They used to store guns in the chicken coop," Henrik went on. "But they're all gone now. I think they took them to Jerusalem."

Henrik didn't explain who *they* were, but Dov had a pretty good idea. *They* were the soldiers of the *Irgun,* the radical Jewish group that had already caused so much trouble over the past few months. *They* were the ones who would rather blow up buildings first, then ask if anyone was inside later. Not that Dov wanted the guns around, but he wondered how much of a defense they could make with just barbed wire, trenches, and an ancient cannon that probably didn't even work.

"Does anybody know how to use that thing?" Dov pointed his thumb at the cannon.

Henrik grinned and shook his head. "Looks pretty iffy to me, too. I don't think it's been working for a hundred years. Good thing we're not relying on it."

Dov dug deeper, faster, keeping the pace like a clock.

" 'Some trust in chariots . . .' " *Clink.* Henrik dug deeper, too. " '. . . and some in horses . . . but we trust in the name of the Lord our God.' "

Leave it to Henrik to slip a Bible verse into the conversation. But for once his choice happened to make a lot of sense. Dov tried to imagine what it might be like to trust in someone else. Someone much bigger than he now felt. Wouldn't it be nice if he could trust the way Henrik did?

Forget it. Instead, Dov lost himself in keeping up the pace, trying to imagine the Egyptians coming at them on horses and chariots. He feared they might come at the kibbutz with something a little more modern, though, and the thought made his blood run cold. His shovel clanked against Henrik's.

"Whoa, there." Henrik moved back a step. "Don't kill yourself. Pace it. We still have a few more hours to finish this."

Dov looked down the line at the others. Besides Henrik and Emily, a half dozen dirt-covered *kibbutzniks* drew closer from the right. About ten others labored in a trench on their left, dirt flying. And of course Julian.

"Look at him!" Henrik smiled at the dog. "He's digging as much as we are."

Not quite. But Julian was still making a go of it, bravely kicking up dirt with the best of them. What dog didn't dream of being *asked* to dig?

"That's a good Jewish dog, there," shouted a man from the other trench.

"Looking for a kosher bone, I hope," replied another.

Everyone laughed at the jokes, but they were like smiles at a funeral: The jokes only masked the tears just below the surface. Dov guessed they all felt the same panic, the same feeling that if they looked over their shoulders, the soldiers would suddenly arrive at the gate. Even David Levin looked especially nervous; he'd taken up a spot in the east watchtower, staring into the distance with his binoculars and not speaking with anyone.

"They're coming," Dov mumbled, not slowing. He meant the Egyptians. Who would deny it as they dug there throughout the rest of the day for a bone that remained just out of reach?

It was true that for every minute he stayed there on the kibbutz, Dov came another minute closer to being trapped there with them—behind the barbed wire and across from the guns of an invading army. What was he doing down there in a trench, digging, when he should already be hurrying north on the road to Tel Aviv?

QUESTIONS
WITHOUT
ANSWERS

Early the next morning, Emily wandered about the kibbutz, watching everyone still bustling about, as if they were preparing for a festival. After digging trenches until three in the morning, she might have slept till noon. But no, her aching arm and back muscles would not let her. Anyway, perhaps there was something else she could do to help.

And this was certainly no festival. Not with sandbags and ditches, barbed-wire fences and blockades. Two stern-faced guards stood by the front gate on the west, the direction of the ocean, and the smaller east gate, which looked toward Jerusalem and the hills.

If we don't get going soon . . . She crossed her arms and shivered despite the growing early morning heat. A team of three young men stood around the old field cannon, trying to make it fire. So far no one had heard the least rumble of success.

"I still say the charge should go in the other way," said one, his voice strained and hoarse. Obviously no one else had slept much, either. His red-eyed companions waved their arms in disagreement.

David Levin, on the other hand, still held his position at the railing up in the east guard tower. For a moment he lowered his binoculars and stared down at Emily, unblinking. She shivered but raised a hand in greeting. He nodded back and returned to his watch. What made him worry so?

Emily finally made her way toward the cookhouse, where several girls about her age were scurrying out with plates of food—food for the trench diggers, who were nearly done, and food for the guards at the gates, at the watchtower, and around the fencing. There was food for all the others, too—people like Matthias, who seemed to have a hundred chores to do before the invasion.

"I wish I could do something else," she sighed just as Henrik came out with a plate in each hand. One was piled high with boiled eggs, the other with bread and cheese.

"Breakfast is served!" he called to her. "Have you had anything to eat yet, Emily?"

Emily had to admit that a spot of breakfast sounded heavenly. She shook her head weakly and accepted a small plate.

"Thank you. I should get something for the dog, too."

"Already done." Henrik smiled back and nodded in the direction of the hen house. "My mother fed him. Hope that's all right. She's also getting some more eggs for you, plus grain, honey, onions, cheese, potatoes, and a few vegetables. We'll have your rescue donkeys packed up and ready to go in no time."

"But . . ." she began. "Can you spare all that food?"

"Food is the one thing we have plenty of." Henrik waved his hand around the kibbutz. "Who else is there to send it to? All our regular markets are closed right now, or at least the roads are. If you don't take this stuff, it'll go bad. Unless your dog eats it all."

"Well, in that case . . ." She took one of the big platters from his hand and helped him carry the food down the path toward a cluster of trench diggers. The exhausted workers stumbled their way, shovels over their shoulders. Emily recognized Dov in the middle, covered with as much dirt as any of them. His canteen, the one David Levin had given him, dangled by a strap around his neck. He raised his eyes as they drew closer.

"We're done," he told them, a weary but odd glow in his eyes. "The trenches on the south side are all dug."

An older man walking next to Dov slapped him on the back.

"He's a human steam shovel, he is!"

The others laughed. Even Dov.

"You make me feel guilty for sleeping the last couple of hours," replied Henrik. He studied Dov, perhaps seeing the same change Emily had noticed. Or maybe it was just her imagination. "I thought you were taking a break like the rest of us."

Dov shook his head and shrugged. "I just wanted to finish the job before I left."

"Midmorning?" Henrik turned to Emily. "Your supplies will be ready by then. I think you two should be going as soon as you can."

The words stopped Dov in his tracks; he closed his eyes and leaned on the handle of his shovel.

"Us two?" he asked, and his voice sounded barely above a whisper. Emily could see his hand trembling as he undid the stopper on his canteen and took another swig of water.

"We're not sending Emily back to Jerusalem alone." Henrik sounded sure as a drill sergeant. "I just assumed since you came with her, you'd be going—"

"I *can't*." Dov's eyes popped open. "I have to get to Tel Aviv to see my mother."

"I understand." Emily held up her hand. "It's all right, really it is."

Henrik looked from the one to the other. "You're welcome to stay at Yad Shalom, of course, until the roads open. But really, there's nothing much else to do here except wait for the soldiers to come."

"And when they do?" Emily asked.

"Maybe they won't. Maybe they'll think it's too much trouble.

But you know how the cities need more time to prepare, and we're the first line of defense."

"Then perhaps we should stay and help after all," suggested Emily.

"No! God brought you here for a reason. There's no doubt you have to take the food back."

Emily paused for a moment, then nodded. It was just that when she'd first thought of bringing the food back across the mountains, somehow she had not imagined it would be alone.

Dov chewed on a piece of bread and watched them.

"You two are always so sure of things," he finally mumbled, but it didn't sound like a complaint.

Emily didn't quite understand what he meant. "Sure of things?" she asked. "Name one."

"Oh, you're sure God brought you here for a reason. Sure that God wants you to bring food back to Jerusalem. Sure about . . . all that." He paused for a moment to take another bite of the flatbread.

Henrik caught Emily's eye for just a moment, as if to ask, "Shall I answer him, or would you like to?" But she turned away, not sure how to explain. She knew that she believed many of the same things Henrik did. But how to explain her faith to a Jewish boy who had been through what Dov had?

"None of it makes any sense, does it?" Henrik asked.

Dov kept chewing. "I asked *you.*"

"That's right, you did." The famous smile returned. "So I'll tell you. I'm not always as sure as I act. Before my friend Peter Andersen introduced me to the Messiah, I was totally lost. Now, I still don't have all the answers. But a few, maybe. I know I can trust God."

"Andersen? Your friend wasn't Jewish?"

Obviously *Andersen* wasn't a good Jewish name.

Henrik shook his head. "No, but—"

"So what would he know about anything? I thought you were talking about something Jewish."

"We *are*, Dov," Emily put in. "After all, Jesus *was* Jewish, you know. He—"

"No, wait a minute." Dov put up his hands to cut her off. "I'm sorry I asked. Every time that name comes up, it makes me feel like some kind of *traitor* just for talking about it."

Emily could tell Dov aimed the last words straight at Henrik, like a spear.

Traitor.

She knew what Dov had probably been told dozens of times: *Jews don't believe in Jesus.* If you did, you wandered over to the wrong camp and betrayed your people, your family, your history.

"Dov." Henrik tried once more. "I know how you feel. I used to think the same—"

"No, you don't know how I feel!" Dov exploded, his cheeks turning cherry red. "*No one* knows how I feel. No one!"

"Well, you asked." Henrik raised his hands in surrender.

But Dov threw down his shovel and stalked away toward the far end of the kibbutz, toward the chicken coop and the animal pens. He whistled for the dog and kicked a rock that hit the side of the coop with a *crack*.

"Honestly!" Emily huffed. "We were just trying to help. He needn't act like such a twit."

Henrik only watched Dov march away, while Emily noticed David Levin looking down from the tower.

Henrik's eyes followed hers. "I wish I knew what that strange fellow was up to," he said.

Emily wasn't sure if Henrik meant David Levin or Dov, and she wasn't sure she wanted to ask.

What is wrong with me? Dov kicked again at the dirt, sending a spray of gravel into the no-man's-land beyond the barbed-wire fence. *Why do I get so worked up about this?*

The questions hounded him. And though they weren't the same as the accusing voice, still he could not escape them or shake them from his mind. They clung, like burrs on socks, to his heart.

Would he really be a traitor to believe as Henrik or Emily did? As Mr. Bin-Jazzi had? He thought back to the kind old Arab man in Jerusalem who had taken Dov in when he'd needed a place to stay. And he could not forget the endless hours when Bin-Jazzi had told him about the man Arab Christians called *Isa al-Masih.*

Yeshua, the Messiah, Jesus. Were they all talking about the same man? The same God? More questions, more burrs on his heart. Dov wished he knew. And for a moment he wished he could believe the way Mr. Bin-Jazzi had.

But no. He just could not betray his people this way. Everyone knew Jews would not, could not follow Yeshua. Not even if it was . . . true. He leaned against the back of the chicken coop, listening to the birds worrying and cackling. He had to get away from the kibbutz.

I'll see my mother soon. Then everything will be fine, he told himself, only half believing. The way things had turned out, could he make it there alone? He'd once thought it would be easy to walk there from Jerusalem, maybe catch a ride. Seeing David Levin step down from the watchtower gave him an idea, and he followed him quietly to the man's tent.

"Mr.—" he began to say, but the words didn't quite leave his mouth. Instead, he paused outside the flap, staring.

Inside, David Levin sat on his cot and cradled his canteen almost the way a father would cradle a newborn. He checked the cap but didn't open it, and Dov remembered that he had *never* seen the man open this canteen.

Odd. Dov held back and watched quietly.

Although Levin's side was turned to the narrow opening, Dov could plainly make out how his lips moved, as if he was *talking* to it. Dov watched the strange sight.

Very odd. Dov still held back as David Levin held the canteen up, chuckled plainly, and patted it on the side.

"You and me, my friend," he told the canteen. "We'll show them."

Show them what? Dov was about to make a noise to announce himself, when Levin slowly lowered the canteen and carefully replaced it under his bed. Dov backed away a couple of steps, quietly, and walked away as David Levin reemerged into the morning light.

"Hey, Dov!"

Dov flinched. He couldn't just walk away.

LAST WARNING

12

"Glad I ran into you." David Levin seemed to be in one of his better moods. "I need to talk to you for a second."

"Me?" Dov looked around, pointing a thumb to his chest, even though they were the only ones there between the tents.

"Of course you. You're still planning to go to Tel Aviv with that big dog of yours, aren't you?"

"Maybe." Dov shrugged. Why should he tell this odd duck more than he already had?

But Levin grabbed Dov's shoulder, swiveled him around, and stared straight into his eyes. Dov could not escape the glare.

"All right. Now, hear what I tell you."

"Ow. My shoulder."

Levin did not ease up, even when Dov tried to squirm free. Where was Julian when you needed him?

"You helped me once, so I'm going to give you a break."

"You're going to break my shoulder if you don't let go."

Levin ignored him.

"I'm serious. You need to leave this kibbutz right now. Today."

"You've seen the Egyptian army?" Dov managed to squeak out the words.

"Not yet." He shook his head. "But I'm talking about *before* tonight. Understand?"

"Sure, I understand." Dov nodded, and Levin let go of his shoulder. "Julian and I were just leaving anyway."

"Fine." Levin held up his finger. "But this is only for your ears, all right? Nobody else."

"Sure thing." Dov felt confused. What kind of crazy warning was this? "But . . . are you leaving, too?"

Levin began to walk away, probably back to the watchtower. He had his binoculars, after all. He paused for a moment, looked back over his shoulder, and sighed.

"Listen, I'll get you out of here. Meet me at seven o'clock at the east gate. Understand?"

"Sure. Seven at the east gate."

"Not a minute earlier, not a minute later. Don't stand around waiting. And not a word to anyone else, not even to your girl-friend."

"She's not my—"

"Save it." David Levin turned on his heel and was gone. At least he hadn't said anything about not bringing the dog.

Not that Dov had wanted to travel any farther with David Levin, but maybe this was his only way to reach Tel Aviv. He would take it.

Then the strange sight came back to him of the man talking to his canteen, like some kind of pet.

He supposed it could contain some kind of liquor. But he'd never seen Levin drink it. Not a drop.

And Dov could not shake the feeling that whatever Levin was hiding had something to do with that canteen.

But how could he know for sure?

Emily tightened up the strap on the side of the donkey. She'd already tightened it twice before that afternoon, but even Dov was doing the same thing before checking the basket of eggs packed in sawdust.

"Are you sure these eggs aren't going to break?" he asked her.

"I told you, Dov, Henrik's mother packs them like this all the time. They'll be okay."

"At least that's what they say."

She looked at him curiously. Hadn't he said he was leaving later that evening for Tel Aviv? What did he care?

"I was just thinking." He wiggled another of the baskets, the one full of green beans. "What about when you get to the place where you were fired on? Remember that village? Are you and Henrik going to know what to do?"

"I assure you, we'll be quite safe. Henrik and Yitzak are going with me. I'm familiar with the path, and we plan to stay as hidden as possible."

"That's what you say." Dov frowned. "But this time you're going to have two donkeys, and you'll be loaded down with supplies. You'll be easier to notice, and you won't be able to move as quickly."

That was true, and they both knew it. But why was Dov pointing this out?

He chewed his lip as he continued to check the animals' loads. Six o'clock, and they were ready to go. They need only wait for darkness.

Dov's stomach would not stop churning—no matter how many times he tried to take a deep breath or tell himself to think of something else, like what the kibbutz might be serving for dinner that evening. After saying good-bye, he had dragged slowly away from where Henrik and Emily had been packing the donkeys, on the safe side of the main gate. To his surprise, he found himself thinking of ways to stay, to avoid Levin and his mysterious canteen.

But how else will I get to Tel Aviv? He's my best chance to get to Cyprus right now. Of course, he could try to make it on his own. Maybe he could do it.

Or maybe not.

Still, he hung back in the growing shadows behind the chicken coop, trying to hear what Henrik was telling his mother and stepfather.

"Yitzak and I will turn right around as soon as we deliver her safely to Jerusalem. We'll be home before the Egyptians arrive, I promise."

"You can't promise something you have no control over," Henrik's mother scolded him.

"I know, I know. But having Yitzak along will help, don't you think?"

Yitzak was one of the bachelors in the kibbutz, a strong-armed young Romanian Jew with a thick black beard. His help was a good thing, Dov supposed. He held back and watched, remembering how he'd spied on Levin earlier that day. Henrik hugged his mother, and Matthias pulled them around with his long arms as they bowed their heads in some kind of prayer.

What was he saying? Dov leaned closer to hear. But no matter how hard he strained his ears, he could make out only the occasional word. "Protect" and "blessing," words one might expect in a prayer. "Emily" and . . .

Was that *his* name? Why would they be praying for him? But he couldn't be sure, and a moment later the huddle was broken and Henrik's parents left. Dov drew back in the shadows as Emily hurried by, headed from the dining hall area. Had she gone to get more food? In any case, it was nearly time for him to leave. Good thing no one could see him blink back the tears that came un-invited to his eyes.

Stop it! He wiped his eyes fiercely on his shirt sleeve, glad for the cover of gathering darkness. No one would see such a mushy thing. Dov did not stop to turn around when it sounded as if Emily made some kind of announcement.

"What do you *mean* he can't come with us? He *told* me he would." Henrik's words sounded startled.

Emily replied something about a girl—a good reason, perhaps. But Dov couldn't worry about what was happening to Emily's plans. No matter what, he was committed to leaving the kibbutz with Levin. Half an hour from now they would simply slip out of the east gate and be on their way. He'd put Julian on a leash, no whimpers, no barks. Easy as that.

Dov retreated to wait in the shadows near Levin's tent, waiting for a sign that it was time to go. He had no watch, but he knew it was growing close to seven o'clock. One question still nagged at him, and he had to know the answer, especially if he was going to place his life in this man's hands once more. What if Levin had been drinking or something like that? Yes, Dov had to know. It only made sense.

What's so special about that canteen of his?

What indeed? Now that the night shadows hid his moves, he had one last chance to find out before they left. His mind made up, Dov crept between tents to where Levin had been sleeping, pulled back the flap, and slipped inside.

His eyes were already adjusted to the darkness, even the near black of the tent. He knelt next to the cot, just as he'd seen Levin do earlier that day, and felt for the canteen. One sniff would tell him what this strange man was up to.

A pair of socks, a coffee cup . . . there! He felt the familiar outline of the canteen, a twin of the one hanging from his own shoulder. Levin's canteen was full; it barely sloshed in Dov's hands.

And then he heard footsteps, close behind the tent.

No time! Without thinking, he slipped his own canteen off his shoulder and replaced it under the cot. And in a catlike move he dove out the door, rolling behind a tuft of thornbushes.

It was Levin, all right. Dov didn't have to wait long to see what would happen. Levin entered the tent and flicked on a lighter, sending the outline of a weird shadow against the tent wall. From his hiding place Dov stared quietly as he watched the man's shadow go through the same moves Dov had just finished. The shadow fell to his knees, felt under the bed, and emerged with Dov's canteen held high like some kind of prize.

Now what?

The flickering light went out, returning them to darkness. A couple of confused chickens warmed up their morning voices. Didn't they realize they were about twelve hours early? Maybe the low rumble of cannon fire miles away had set them on edge. The Egyptians were probably on the march.

But Levin didn't stop to listen. Instead, he slipped out of his tent, keeping to the same shadows Dov had lingered in on his way to the tent. Not knowing what else to do, Dov followed without a sound.

Levin walked straight and silent, as if on a mission. He avoided two knots of young kibbutz workers, slipping around the far sides of several tents. It was clear he knew just where he was going— and just what he wanted to do when he got there. Dov stuck to him like a hidden shadow.

A minute later the man was leaning up against the low rock wall surrounding the kibbutz well, looking around and acting strangely casual. On his knees now against the corner of a tool shed, Dov thought he even heard Levin whistle a Jimmy Dorsey big-band tune.

What's he doing? A bare light bulb from outside another shed cast its lone light on the scene.

Levin looked around one more time, as if checking to be sure he was alone. No one but Dov seemed to be watching as the low thunder of distant guns sounded one more time. Ignoring the sounds, he pulled out Dov's canteen and set it on the edge of the well. He unscrewed the cap nearly all the way, slowly, at arm's length, as if it might explode.

He must think it smells pretty bad.

Levin still didn't open the canteen all the way. Instead, he left it balanced on the edge of the well and retreated several steps. For a moment he kept watch, pausing and crossing his arms when a young girl ran by. When she had passed by, he picked up a stick with his right hand and used it to gently tip the bottle over so that it emptied into the well. With his left hand he covered his nose and mouth.

If he only knew. Dov might have laughed out loud if it weren't so weird. *It's only my water!*

When the canteen had emptied, Levin squinted as he popped it into the well with the end of his stick. Next he tossed the stick into the bushes, lowered the well's wooden cover, and hurried away.

Dov stood for a second in the shadows, staring at the well, trying to figure out what he had just seen.

Maybe he gave up drinking, he told himself, *and that was just his way of dumping his liquor.*

No. Even as Dov replayed the strange scene in his mind, he knew it wasn't so. He knew he'd just seen something evil. And Dov also knew that somehow he'd managed to remove the bullet from Levin's very dangerous weapon. What kind of weapon, he wasn't sure. But now the other canteen—Levin's canteen—hung innocently from Dov's shoulder.

Dov shivered and held the canteen out, well away from his body, as if it might burn him right through the metal and canvas. Whatever Levin had meant to dump into the drinking water, well,

Dov was sure he didn't want to take so much as a sniff of it now. Not after what he'd just seen.

So much for traveling to Tel Aviv with him.

Instead, Dov hurried the other way, straight for the main gate, where the donkeys had been readied. Maybe he could still catch Emily and Henrik.

ESCAPE AND RETREAT

13

At first Henrik walked so quickly that Emily could hardly keep up.

But I mustn't complain, she told herself. Still, she wasn't sure even the donkeys could keep up this pace for long. She held her aching side and did her best to catch her breath.

"Do you need a rest?" Henrik's first words since they left Yad Shalom seemed to echo in the dark hills, though he barely spoke above a whisper.

"You mean me?"

"No, I was talking to Lizzi. Of course you. Do you need a breather?"

"I'm, uh . . ." Emily did her best to cover the sound of gasping.

"All right." Henrik pulled back on the lead donkey's bridle, and Lizzi came to a halt. "Just a couple of minutes, though. We need to put some miles under our feet before morning."

"If that's what you want." Emily brought Laslo to a stop, too. She didn't want to slow them down.

"What was that?" Emily felt herself jump at a rustle of wind and leaves next to the trail.

"Relax." Henrik patted Lizzi's neck. "We have a long way to go. It's nothing."

Nothing? A growing thunder rumbled up from the south.

"That, on the other hand . . ." Henrik didn't have to explain the nearing menace. Emily knew what had to be on his mind as the soldiers came nearer. What would happen to his home? His parents? They had to keep moving so he could return quickly.

"Right, then." She drew herself up and tried not to shiver. Even with the breeze, it wasn't cold that made her tremble. "We should hurry."

This time they talked a little, perhaps to keep their minds on other things than the man-made thunder. As the minutes turned to miles, they spoke of movies they'd like to see, of books they'd read. Henrik told her he'd been trying to read a new book by the American William Saroyan, about a boy named Homer, who delivered telegrams in his town in Kalifornien, and . . .

"Califor*nia,"* she corrected him.

"California. Of course, sorry. My Danish still comes through. The sign for Homer's town reminded me of Denmark."

"Oh?"

" 'Ithaca, California,' " he recited. " 'East, West, Home Is Best. Welcome, Stranger.' "

Emily thought about that for a moment. Charming, but it hardly made sense.

"How does it remind you of Denmark?"

"It's like a Danish saying. *Ude er godt, men hjemme er bedst."*

She waited for the translation.

"Out is good, but home is best."

"I see. Home is best." The saying made her think of the home she no longer had, about Mum and Daddy, who were certainly worried about her by now. Worried sick, if she knew her father. Did her aunt Rachel and uncle Anthony have any clue she was walking across the hills with a young Danish fellow named

Henrik? They would be thankful for the food, of course, but she knew they'd be concerned, even upset, at the risk she was taking.

Oh, she'd made a mess of things this time. That much she knew for certain.

"Emily Parkinson, you surprise me."

"Me?" She wasn't sure how they'd gone from talking about William Saroyan to her.

"Yes, and to tell you the truth, it surprises me you're walking across the mountains with a load of food for a group of orphans."

The statement caught her off guard—and the unspoken question: Why was she doing this?

"I, ah . . ." Emily wasn't sure she could answer. But her mind drifted to the memory of hollow-eyed Jewish refugees crowded on the decks of the *Aliyah*—the same ship from which Dov had escaped. She could not forget the soldiers who had beaten back the refugees. Nor could she forget the settlers on the Yad Shalom kibbutz, hoping desperately to grow peace in their dusty fields. Or the orphans, the fighting . . .

To be sure, beginning a new country was no easy thing.

"I'm sorry." Emily wiped away a tear and wrapped an arm around Laslo's neck. Once more they stopped.

"Don't apologize." Henrik's voice sounded steady and strong. "You're doing the right thing. I'm disappointed Yitzak couldn't come with us after all. But we'll get this food to Jerusalem. You'll see. God is in control."

There, he'd said it again, as he had once said it to Dov: *God is in control.* Was He, truly?

Emily looked down at her feet. She didn't need light to recognize the pain of blisters on blisters or to imagine the scuffs and gashes in what had once been her nicest pair of black-and-white saddle shoes. She let tears follow more tears, and they flashed like tiny diamonds in the night.

God is in control, she told herself, as if repeating the words would convince her. She knew it was true, despite the throbbing of her swollen feet and the thunder that had grown closer. She nodded.

"Yes, I know." Her whisper caught on the dark breeze, along with a hint of far-off voices. Was she just hearing things again? She paused, but all she could hear was the breeze whistling through distant pines. Perhaps they were the voices of history, drifting through the ancient hills of Israel.

Dov knew he was no pathfinder. Not unless picking his way through the war-scarred train yards and bombed-out cities of Europe could be called pathfinding. But following two donkeys east over the hills had not been a huge challenge, even in the dark. After all, he could smell, couldn't he?

Well, if he couldn't, then old Julian still could. Like a hound dog on the scent, he loped along next to Dov. And so they ran, gulping in the night air, pausing once in a while to gasp for breath and make sure they were still on the right trail. Dov still remembered every rocky step of the way that he, Levin, and Emily had come west.

We'll catch up with them. They can't be moving that quickly.

For a reason he didn't understand, he clutched the canteen tightly. He supposed he could have just set it aside or left it behind, but who knew what trouble it might cause. Every once in a while he checked the cap, just to be sure it was on nice and tight. He quickened his pace, sometimes running blindly through flat, rocky meadows that rose gradually toward the distant city. At least Levin was out of the picture.

Dov imagined the man traveling north on the coastal highway, north to Tel Aviv. The way Dov should have been traveling, too.

Isn't that what he said? Dov tried to remember but couldn't as he jogged, faster and faster. Julian fell a couple of strides behind. What if Levin was taking this path to Jerusalem instead? What if Dov now ran into him?

A sound up ahead made him pause for a moment. Voices? That would be either Emily and Henrik, or Levin talking to himself. Or . . .

"Yal-la!" Dov skidded to a stop when he heard the Arabic. He knew those words: *Let's go!*

No! He grabbed Julian around the neck and strained to see in the darkness, to see anything that would tell him he hadn't just heard Egyptian soldiers headed his way. But as he froze behind a boulder, he heard the shouts of several—and he made out the dark shadows of one . . . two . . . three. Maybe more.

That was all he needed to see. Quickly, he wondered how he had missed finding Emily and Henrik. Had he missed their trail? He turned his back to the soldiers, pulled Julian to his side, and sprinted off the only other open way, a little to the right. That had to be their route.

Did they see me? He couldn't be sure. At least no one had shot at him, not yet. But he still had to find Emily and Henrik, or the soldiers would surely overtake them.

"Owwff!" His toe caught a rock, sending him flying, face first, into the dirt. He gasped for the air that had been smacked from his lungs, then felt for the canteen. Still there. He fought his way to his knees, pulling precious air back into his lungs gasp by gasp, feeling like a fish out of water. Behind him a soldier laughed.

Good. They haven't seen me yet. Still, he couldn't waste a moment. A second later he was pounding back down the hills, trying to find the portion of trail he had missed.

Where are they? He ran, sometimes stumbling, then picking himself up again, flying down the hills faster than he should. Julian plodded faithfully along behind him. For how long? Five minutes? Ten? He lost track, until at last a familiar sound caught his ear. He tried to make his legs halt, tried to hear over his own gasping for breath.

"Yah! Come on, Lizzi, you old—"

Dov heard a slap, probably Henrik's hand on the backside of a donkey. Julian yelped, as if he knew they had found their prize. Dov zeroed in on the sound, heading straight for a small gully.

"Emily!" he called, not too loudly. "Are you there?"

They had to be. He stumbled to a stop in front of the donkeys, ready to collapse.

"What in the world?" Henrik grabbed hold and held him up by the arms.

"Dov? Where did you come from?" asked Emily. "And how did you get ahead of us?"

"Forget that." Dov gasped. "I'm telling you . . . they're coming."

"Who are you talking about?" Henrik looked toward Dov. "Who's coming?"

"Egyptian soldiers." Dov finally spit it out. "Must be scouts or whatever. But . . . you've got to listen to me. They're coming this way."

Emily's gasp told him she understood.

"How far did you say?" asked Henrik.

Dov shook his head and swallowed hard. "I don't know exactly. Uh . . . ten minutes down the trail, no more. I was running. I don't—"

"All right." Henrik cut him off and pulled Lizzi around with a yank. "We can't go north or south."

Dark shadows showed the walls of the *wadi,* the dry river canyon they stood in. If they'd kept climbing as they had been, they would meet the soldiers head on. Dov supposed they might be able to climb the canyon walls—if it were light, without the donkeys or the dog, and if they had all day. Right now, though, there was only one way to turn.

"Back to Yad Shalom!" Henrik whispered.

ATTACK ON
YAD SHALOM

14

"What about the donkeys?" Dov asked as they ducked into the dining hall. By that time the rest of the kibbutz had gathered together inside the farm's largest building—parents and their children, grandfathers and grandmothers, unmarried men and women huddled in groups of two and three. A baby began to cry, setting off two others.

"The donkeys will be fine," answered Henrik, but Dov wasn't so sure. How long would they be fine tied up in the thicket of trees just outside the east gate? They had a bucket of water, but what if the Egyptian troops discovered them?

Dov *was* sure there was no way to check on them now. Like it or not, the care and feeding of Lizzi and Laslo wasn't at the top of anyone's list, at least not at the moment.

Matthias raised his hand and whistled for quiet. "All right, everyone. We have just a few minutes. You all heard what the kids saw in the hills, coming our way. And you know our job here."

"Yes," came a young man's voice from the back of the room. "We're the target for their practice."

A few people joined in the nervous chuckle.

"That's not it at all." Matthias pulled a chair closer and stood on it, as if he needed more elevation to make himself heard. "Let me explain it again. Our job is to slow the enemy down as long as we can. We have to give our Haganah boys time to prepare, to gather their forces. That's what the ditches are about, the barbed wire, the—"

"The cannon?" yelled another man. This time everyone laughed, even Matthias.

"I still want to know why they took all our guns!" demanded a voice. The crowd parted enough to let the questioner through.

"We talked about this before, Reuven." Matthias sounded like a patient schoolteacher. "They needed the weapons in Tel Aviv. And—"

Reuven finished the sentence. "And Yad Shalom is too small to bother with."

This time no one said anything. Even the babies were silent. Julian slobbered on the palm of Dov's hand, a friendly gesture if there ever was one. But who had time for a town hall meeting?

"Does the cannon work?" Dov asked.

"We've tried," Matthias said. "It's unreliable. Goes off sometimes, but most times it just goes *ffffitt!*"

"Oh." Dov nodded. "Well, *a* cannon is better than *no* cannon, especially if—"

Everyone else heard the first shell, too. They froze in place as the terrifying scream passed just overhead, then faded. The next moment the floor trembled with the impact. Julian woofed happily, as if it were all part of a grand game.

"Don't panic!" Matthias held up his hands for quiet when everyone erupted into nervous buzzing. Had anyone heard the sound of death raining down on their homes and families the way Dov had? He was sure many had, back in Poland or Germany or Austria or Russia, during the war. There was no mistaking the sound. It was the sound they'd expected ever since hearing news on independence day of the enemy attack.

"All right, everyone!" Matthias had not given up trying to calm people down. "Into the shelter!"

Without argument, all one hundred six members of Kibbutz Yad Shalom hurried for the door.

"Go! Go! Go!" Matthias waved them through. Dov thought it amazing how quickly so many people could move when they wanted to.

"Dov!" Emily caught his eye as they moved toward the bomb shelter that had been dug under the concrete floor of the dining hall. They moved shoulder to shoulder with everyone around them toward the outside shelter entrance on the building's side. "Stay by me?"

He nodded his head and moved through the small sea of people toward her. He held tightly to Julian's collar.

Henrik came up from behind. "We'll stay together," he told them.

Again Dov nodded. That was fine with him.

They all ducked when they heard another incoming shriek, this one even closer. In less time than it took to describe, half the chicken coop exploded into toothpicks and chicken feathers. The eruption sent dozens of terrified survivors squawking into the grassy commons—most flapping their wings wildly, many obviously injured, some turning in senseless circles as if their wings were broken or they had nowhere to run.

And they didn't, as round after round now came shrieking in from the south. Most landed in the fields around the kibbutz, producing sickening thuds and shaking not only the ground but everyone's teeth and nerves, as well.

It's happening all over again. Dov stared in numb horror. Another round slammed into the ground right next to the chicken coop, digging out a small crater. Chickens mixed with dirt to shower the few people not yet in the shelter.

"Quick," Emily yelled, taking Dov by the arm. "Bring Julian!"

Yet another round slammed the garden, filling the air with shredded cucumbers. Dov stumbled backward, horrified and fascinated at the same time. He could not turn away until Henrik and Emily finally helped him down the stairs and shut the heavy double doors behind them. Julian followed them gladly, not a half step behind Dov's heels. Emily rammed home the pin of a lock, as if that would somehow keep the missiles and the soldiers out. But it was all they could do to convince themselves they would be safe.

Someone had lit candles inside the tomb they had dug for themselves, and the dim yellow flames cast wavering shadows on the concrete ceiling. Dov found a place to sit on the hard-packed dirt floor. They listened to the thumps, followed by the shaking, gasping each time, as if the other team had scored another goal. And of course there was nothing they could do to stop the attack.

Another hit shook the ceiling, raining dust on their heads. The three babies wailed, petrified sobs muffled by their mothers' hugs.

Dov didn't move away when he felt Henrik's arm around him.

"We'll be okay down here," Henrik whispered. "Don't forget that God's in—"

"I know, I know," Dov dared interrupt. "God's in control."

Dov sighed and coughed in the stale air. He wasn't sure he had meant the words. Did he believe them, even a little? What else was there to believe? Another hit, and the columns holding up their ceiling shook. If he didn't think Henrik was right, well, he wasn't sure what else he had to choose from.

"Keep praying." Matthias rested his hand gently on Henrik's shoulder as he passed by. Henrik's face brightened for a moment in the candlelight, and he nodded before Matthias continued on.

They wouldn't be the only ones praying as the shelling grew louder and more intense. With each thump they could only hold on to one another and wait for the next. Were they just waiting to die at Kibbutz Yad Shalom?

What a name. Dov closed his eyes and rocked slowly as he

remembered the Hebrew words. *Monument to Peace.* Pretty soon the incoming explosions would turn this monument to a pile of rubble. *Then they can call it Gravestone to Peace.*

Thump! The cries grew a little louder, a little more on edge.

"Let's have a drink of that, young fellow."

Dov felt someone tug at his canteen, *the* canteen. In all the terror, he'd completely forgotten it still hung from his neck. He snapped open his eyes to see an older man, his hands on the canteen. Dov tugged back.

"No!" Dov almost shouted.

The man's eyes widened.

"Now, just wait a minute. This is no time to keep things to yourself."

"You don't understand." Dov didn't let go of the canteen. "There's something in this canteen that's not right."

"What are you talking about?"

"It's a long story. I don't know what's in here for sure, but it's not good."

The next round almost threw them to the ground. But now the older man had his eyes on the prize, and he wasn't giving up that easily.

"Water out here doesn't taste like Coca-Cola. Now, give me the canteen!"

The tug-of-war would have been uglier if Henrik hadn't come to the rescue. But he didn't understand, either.

"Dov, I think you should—"

Dov could have guessed at Henrik's next words, but he didn't get the chance to explain. The entire ceiling shuddered as never before, and for a moment Dov caught a glimpse of starlight above his head.

It all happened too quickly. The explosion. The trembling like an earthquake, only so much worse. The beam. The shout of warning that came too late.

"Dov!" Henrik must have seen the danger. "Look out!"

Instead of diving for safety as he should have done, Henrik dove right into harm's way. Dov felt himself lifted and spun, heard the groaning and splintering of the beam and their concrete roof. And then their cellar shelter collapsed into chaos.

TRUE BETRAYER

15

It's all my fault. Dov squeezed out the hand towel and daubed Henrik's clammy forehead. What good it would do for someone as badly hurt as Henrik, he didn't know. He'd seen Emily do the same, though, when it was her turn to watch. And for the past forty hours, they'd done plenty of watching.

Praying, too. For what seemed like the first time in his life, Dov prayed, long and hard. Sitting there gave him plenty of time to do that. It actually wasn't the first time. He'd prayed once or twice before. Only then, it had always been for himself: *Help me quick, God!* Now he prayed for Henrik.

At least God had answered part of their prayer. Henrik was still alive after they'd pulled him out of the rubble. Alive, but just barely. Both his legs had been badly crushed by the falling beam, he'd taken a nasty blow to the head, and several ribs were probably cracked. Even so, he breathed slowly but evenly, and he opened his eyes every few hours to give them a weak smile before going back to sleep. Matthias had told them it was a miracle they'd been able to get him out of there alive. Two others had not been so lucky.

If Dov had believed in luck, then he'd been dealt more than his share. Because when Henrik shoved him out of the way of the falling beam, he'd spared Dov and taken the full force of the blow.

"It should have been me," Dov told Henrik for the tenth time, as if complaining to a sleeping, half-dead hero would make any difference. But everyone knew it was true. To his own surprise, Dov told himself he would have given anything to have traded places with Henrik. That foreign thought invaded his me-first thinking and filled him with guilt.

"It should have been me," he repeated. At least the cursed canteen had been buried in the rubble, far out of reach and hopefully lost for good.

Julian opened one eye from his spot on the tent floor, only to close it again.

"Hey, there." The words made Dov jump, sending the hand towel flying.

Henrik's eyes were open again.

"Oh, wow," Dov stammered. "You're awake. I'll . . . I'll go get your parents."

Dov stood to leave the tent but was stopped by the brush of Henrik's hand on his arm.

"No, wait." Henrik looked up at him. "Stay."

Henrik's eyes searched Dov's face. "Tell me what happened. I feel like . . . I've been run over by a truck."

A lump began to rise in Dov's throat, and he wasn't sure he would be able to explain.

"It was no truck, Henrik. An Egyptian shell hit the shelter. Do you remember anything about what happened?"

"I'm starting to. Where are the Egyptians now?"

"I don't know. Nobody else does, either. After the roof fell on us, they stopped shooting."

"Fantastic. When was that?"

"About a day and a half ago. Almost two, I guess."

"I've been snoozing this whole time?"

"Off and on."

"God's in control."

"Okay, Henrik. You've said that before. But look, I need to tell you something."

"I'm not going anywhere." Henrik had closed his eyes again. Maybe he had spent all his strength.

"I have to tell you . . ." Dov's thoughts tangled and twisted like spaghetti.

"Go ahead."

"Everybody knows it should have been me who got crushed under that beam."

"Should have been you," Henrik repeated with his eyes closed, his voice faded to the weakest of whispers. "But it wasn't."

"And I just feel really bad about what happened."

"You don't know how *I* feel."

Was that a joke? The corners of Henrik's mouth had curled up.

"Anyway, what I'm trying to say is, you saved my life, and . . ." Henrik held up his hand.

"Believe me, I didn't plan it this way. So don't thank me."

"Don't thank you? Why not?"

Maybe it was the pain-killer they'd given Henrik from the first-aid kit, but he wasn't making sense anymore. At least he opened his eyes.

"You're going to die someday anyway. Right?"

"Well . . . I suppose." Dov hadn't thought of it that way. Even all those years during the war, when he saw death every day with his own eyes, it was always someone else. Not him. Not yet.

"But let's say I really *did* save your life." Now Henrik's eyes were clear and searching, and Dov squirmed. "Would you accept what I did?"

"Accept it?" Dov didn't quite follow.

"Yes, would you accept what happened?"

What was Henrik trying to say?

"How could I not?"

"Exactly." The voice faded further. "So listen to this."

Dov bent closer, until his face hovered just inches from Henrik's. It was the only way to hear his friend's weak whisper.

"Maybe I took your place under that beam. I don't know. But I do know your Messiah really did take your place. He died for you, Dov. Why don't you believe that?"

"I'm afraid of being a traitor. Of . . . betraying my people." Dov clamped his eyes shut and started to pull back, but Henrik had reached up and hooked a finger around the Star of David hanging around Dov's neck. The Magen David with the cross inside. Dov had to grip the cot frame to keep from falling forward.

"Listen!" Henrik insisted. "You're no traitor. You're just scared . . . and stubborn. I was, too. But you've heard everything you need to know now, and you need to decide what you believe. Next time I may not be there to shove you out of harm's way. Please, Dov. If you accept what I did for you, now accept something a lot better."

Henrik's hand fell back to his bandaged chest, but still Dov couldn't move. He listened to his friend's shallow, steady breathing and tried to make sense of what Henrik had said. Then he dropped to his knees next to the cot, right next to Julian, to pray once more.

"How long do we just sit here?" Reuven brought his challenge to the huddled meeting that night. "The wolves are circling."

He's right about that, thought Emily. She looked around at the small crowd gathered in the clearing between the bombed-out chicken coop and another barn. Emily was shaking as much as anyone.

"I know you feel like a target." Matthias lifted his hands. "But—"

"You better believe we do," replied Reuven. "We should have just painted a sign on the roof, eh? Hit Me Here would have worked just fine."

"All right, we're still holding up. We've slowed them down at least two days. That's what we're here for."

"Yes, I've heard that before. Well, I still say we'd have been much better off if the British had allowed us to bring in more of our own weapons." The man looked over at Emily as he spoke, as if she had been personally responsible for that decision.

"You keep her out of this." Dov stepped up, but Emily tried to hold him back.

"That's quite all right," she told him. "My father, Major Parkinson, tried to keep order as much as he could when he was here. I daresay it was no simple matter."

"Your father!" Reuven wasn't finished. "And where is he now, eh, miss? Running back to London with his tail tucked between his legs, right? Back where he belonged in the first place. Back where *you* belong!"

"That's ENOUGH!" thundered Matthias. "Emily came here to help people, in case you haven't heard. Fighting amongst ourselves isn't going to help anyone."

And neither is insulting Daddy that way. Emily tried to keep her lip from trembling and the tears from filling her eyes.

"Ahh!" Reuven turned on his heel and pushed his way into the darkness.

"I'm sorry, Emily," Dov told Emily, and the words startled her. *He's sorry?* What had gotten into him? She tried to make out the expression on his face, but it had grown too dark.

"It's settled, then." Matthias sounded as if he was ready to wrap up the meeting. "We stay put. We keep the gates locked, and we keep the cannon loaded. All in favor?"

Most of the crowd mumbled a quiet "aye." Only a few said "nay."

"Good." Matthias clapped his hands together. "Simha and Aaron have watchtower duty again. Let us know if the soldiers get any close—"

"Matthias! Matthias!" A young man burst in on the meeting as he sprinted down the path. "Someone's at the front gate, and he wants to be let in!"

"Who is it?"

"Not sure. He's dressed like an Arab, and he says he'll only talk to you."

Meeting over. No one wasted any time running to the front gate to see.

"Hold on!" yelled Matthias. "The guards on duty will take care of this. It won't take everyone in the kibbutz."

Of course no one listened, so there was nothing to do but join the parade. Sure enough, a man in flowing white robes stood behind the double-wide wire gate, arms crossed and feet planted wide. He didn't flinch when the gate guard aimed a flashlight beam squarely in his face, but he did scowl at the sound of Julian's deep-throated barks. Despite the man's strangely darkened complexion, no one could doubt who stood waiting to be let in.

David Levin.

"What in the world?" Matthias stood behind the gate with his hands planted on his hips, staring at the unexpected visitor. Dov and Emily held back behind Matthias, in his shadow.

"I don't have time to explain, Karlsson," said Levin. "Just—"

"But what are you doing in a *kaffiyeh* and Arab robes?"

Levin sighed and leaned closer, ready to tell his secret. "You know I work for the Haganah. Sometimes we just need to check up on our neighbors."

Yet Matthias didn't move, as if he was trying to decide what this meant.

Levin pointed a finger through the chain link. "Come on, will you? Hold the dog back and open . . . this . . . gate!"

Finally Matthias nodded to one of the guards to unlock the padlocked chain, while another swung the gate open. Dov looped a hand through Julian's collar as Levin wasted no time hurrying inside. He stopped only a stride in front of them and reached beneath his robe.

"Step aside, please," said the guard who had opened the gate. He was ready to swing it shut again as quickly as he could.

But Levin didn't budge. "As bad as it might look, my friends," he told them in a low, steady voice, "you're going to have to trust me."

"Pardon?" Matthias didn't understand. Neither did anyone else. "Trust you? Whatever do you mean?"

"I mean that what happens next is for the good of Eretz Israel. You will command your people not to resist, and all will be well. Please believe me. Everything is not as it seems."

Emily had never seen such a storm cloud cross the face of Matthias Karlsson. But she now understood the reason for the fire in his eyes—the ugly, snub-nosed weapon Levin gripped in his right hand.

FRIENDLY TRAITOR

16

David Levin's odd words and evil-looking gun were obviously just the introduction. In an instant a troop of uniformed Egyptian soldiers with drawn rifles trotted out of the darkness and in through the gate.

The kibbutz guard didn't have a chance to aim his ancient rifle before he was confronted by three soldiers, one on every side. All he could do was lay down his weapon. Emily wasn't sure it worked, anyway.

"I can't believe you would do such a thing!" cried Matthias, but Levin refused to look him in the eye.

The entire operation had obviously been planned right down to the second. Rifles ready, each grim-faced soldier took up position inside the gate, opening the way for more to arrive. By now the thunder had arrived in full and brutal force. And David Levin the Jew had become David Levin the Arab spy.

"This way! *Yamin!* To the right!" He hurled instructions at the soldiers in their own language, too fast for Emily to catch most of the words. She caught the meaning, though. With a hurry-up motion of his hand, Levin pointed the way for a steady stream of helmeted soldiers to enter and take control.

Never mind what Levin had told them about trust. Kibbutz Yad Shalom had just been handed over to the invaders. And unless one counted the off-and-on shelling over the past two days, it had happened without a shot. They'd been betrayed by one of their own, or someone they'd thought was one of their own. Levin looked as if he'd perhaps smeared dark lotion on his skin to look more like an Arab. But who could be sure anymore?

"I see it, but I still don't believe it," Dov whispered. While Matthias had been escorted somewhere else, they had been rounded up with a handful of others who'd been watching near the gate and forced to stand against the dining hall's one remaining wall. It had all happened so quickly. Now they were guarded by a young, gum-chewing soldier wearing a helmet that fell over his ears and nearly covered his dark, unsearchable eyes. Dov had tied the end of Julian's leash to a pipe near the outside of the building, but he obviously couldn't keep the dog from growling.

The growls made no difference. Dozens more soldiers came rushing in, followed by several transports, officers' cars, even a half-track truck with a large machine gun mounted in back. Where had they all come from, and so suddenly? The awful blue-black smoke belching from each truck rasped at the inside of Emily's throat like sandpaper and made her gag. She noticed that Dov tried to shield his mouth with a hand, but of course it was no good. She couldn't seem to stop coughing as the invasion continued. Coughing and shivering.

"You okay?" Dov asked her quietly.

Obviously she was not, but she was no worse off than anyone else, so she nodded. "Just a bit of smoke. I'll be all right in a minute."

But even after a few minutes, her hands still shook, in spite of the balmy May evening air. She felt as powerless to stop shaking as she had been to stop the soldiers from marching into Yad Shalom.

Dov rested a hand on her shoulder. "Relax," he whispered. "I've lived through this kind of thing before. And you know what Henrik is always saying."

She glanced over at him for a moment in surprise.

"God is in control." He barely moved his lips, as if the words had been spoken by some kind of ventriloquist, and he a puppet on a string. This was Dov?

Emily started to shiver once again as Levin marched over to their group, his robes flowing in the night.

"You!" The man brushed off the Egyptian guard and pointed at Dov. "Come with me."

Dov kept his arms crossed and his expression cold as Levin dragged him by the arm to a quiet corner by the fence. So much for their work on the trenches. What would the soldiers use them for now? Garbage dumps? Latrines?

"Play along with me." Levin spoke to him in Hebrew out of the corner of his mouth. "They won't understand us."

A couple of soldiers going the other way nodded and saluted.

"I don't want to take any chances. Do you get my meaning?"

"Sure, I get your meaning." Dov gritted his teeth and shook his arm free. White-hot fury steamed his ears and made red spots dance in the corners of his vision. He wondered what he could do to this traitor, given the chance. If he could just find a rock, it might be big enough to . . .

But then another thought seeped into his mind, a strange, foreign thought. He realized that he actually felt sorry for Levin.

Sorry? For such a low traitor? Why?

"What did you say?" Dov realized Levin had been speaking, but the words had brushed by his ears without going in.

Levin cocked his head to the side.

"What's wrong with you, kid? First you didn't come with me—not that I care. Now I'm telling you one more time how to get out of this place, and you're daydreaming."

As much as he hated to, Dov focused on the man's face once again.

"All right, then." Levin seemed satisfied. "You look fine. Been drinking from the well?"

Here it comes. Dov raised an eyebrow and tried to think of a safe answer. Something to keep Levin talking and that wouldn't give away what Dov already knew.

"Not for a couple of days. I have a bottle in my tent."

True. He did.

"You don't know how lucky you are. Now, just tell me when people started getting sick."

"Sick?" Dov shook his head. "No one's sick, except maybe Mrs. Gruenbaum. She was sneezing all over the place yesterday and complaining about her arthritis. Does that count?"

Levin sighed, exasperated. His eyes darted about, watching anyone who passed by.

"Don't tell me no one is sick. I left here about forty-eight hours ago, and people aren't sick?"

Dov shrugged and shook his head. "I got sick to my stomach when I saw what kind of traitor you are."

It was true. What more could this man do to them?

For a moment Levin raised his hand as if to strike.

I'm not going to move, Dov told himself, and he steeled his shoulders for the hit. *Go ahead.*

But Levin changed his mind, folded his fingers, and instead pointed at Dov's face.

"I'm going to tell you this once, and once only. You want to know why?"

"Looks like I'm going to hear it, either way."

"I still owe you one. As strange as it may sound to you right now, I still have a sense of honor."

"Hmm." Dov wondered what might have happened if he and Emily had not helped this traitor. At least they wouldn't be having this conversation.

"And I am *not* a traitor."

"You could have fooled me."

"Exactly." He paused for a moment, and a dry smile crept across his lips. "You think I work for the Egyptians. And the Egyptians think I work for the Egyptians."

"Something about the headgear." Dov stuck out his chin to show he was not afraid.

"Believe what you want. I don't care. But let me just tell you one thing. If you want to get out of this forsaken place alive, don't go near the well, got it? Go thirsty, but don't go near the well."

"What's wrong with the well?" Dov had a pretty good guess by now. "Was it that stuff you dumped in it?"

Levin blinked in utter surprise, as if he himself had been slapped across the cheek. But only a moment.

Dov gave him credit. *He's a good actor.*

"Oh, so you've been playing a little spy game, have you?"

"What was in the canteen?" Dov decided to take a chance. "Poison?"

"Well, well. You really are a natural spy. Too bad you're not a few years older. We could use a few more good men. Still, you'll get a chance in the next war to serve your country. Believe me, this is just the beginning."

"You still haven't answered about the canteen."

Levin studied Dov's face for a few moments, and Dov did his best not to blink.

"Do you know what typhus and dysentery are?"

"That's what was in your canteen? Typhus and dysentery germs?"

"Enough to infect a small army."

This army, Dov guessed.

Levin went on to boast about his horrible plan. "Takes just two or three days to bring them to their knees. I'm quite surprised no one is sick yet."

Dov swallowed hard. He wasn't sure what typhus or dysentery were, exactly. But they sounded bad. So *that's* what he had been carrying around. But that also meant—

"That proves who you are!" Dov felt his temperature rising again. "You would dump that stuff into our well without telling anyone. You would have let us die! Why?"

"There was no other way. This is a war, in case you haven't noticed. People die in wars. The innocent along with the enemy."

"You didn't have to—"

"I *did* have to, or many more would be killed. Don't you see? These people here were in the line of fire. They were going to die anyway. For Eretz Israel."

"You don't know that."

"I *do* know that. And it had to be a secret, or the Egyptians wouldn't be drinking from the well right now."

"But—" Dov still couldn't believe what he was hearing.

"If it makes you feel any better, it wasn't meant for you. I offered to get you out of here, didn't I?" He paused once more as another pair of soldiers walked by. "It's meant for them."

"Why should I believe you?"

"Have I told *them* about the well?"

"I don't know. Have you?"

"Come with me and see for yourself." With that, he grabbed Dov's arm and marched toward the well.

"One last warning. Don't think you can be heroic. Our secret stays our secret."

"And what if I warn everybody?"

"Oh, I don't think you'll do that."

"You don't know me."

"I don't need to."

Dov still wasn't sure whose side Levin was on, but he still felt sorry for him. At the same time, he felt like kicking him in the shins. Hard.

"Think about it for a minute. You can make it out of here alive. But if you say a word, the Egyptians won't drink the water. Instead, they're going to make *you* drink it, and all your friends, too. You understand what I'm saying?"

Dov understood, all right. He would keep his secret about the switched canteens. But even knowing the well wasn't poisoned, he had no way of telling what lay ahead for him at the Yad Shalom well.

DECISION AT
THE WELL

17

Emily could tell something important was happening at the well. Besides all the extra trucks, at least fifty more soldiers had formed a ring around the area. And despite the floodlights that had been strung, she could not see the raised stone well.

Whatever is happening?

She heard Arabic voices, including one she thought might be Levin's, who was also speaking rapidly in Arabic. Something about this being the deepest well in the area, the best water for their troops, and a reward for delivering it into their hands. If they would just slow down and not slur their words so much, Emily thought she might be able to understand more.

In any case, the main speaker had to be Levin, the betrayer. This same man she and Dov had helped across the mountains now turned around and helped the invaders destroy what was left of Kibbutz Yad Shalom. They all seemed to take great delight in the twin bonfires that were once the trim little chicken coop and the meeting hall. As flames licked higher and higher, she heard laughing and backslapping. Mission accomplished.

"What are they going to do with us?" Emily worried aloud. By the expressions on the faces around her, she wasn't the only one worried.

"I've heard the Arabs take no prisoners," murmured a woman, but Emily didn't even want to *think* about what she had said. It was too . . .

"Everything will be all right," Henrik said to Emily, but even he could not hide the wrinkle of doubt in his forehead. At least he was sitting up, though of course he still could not move much or walk. In all the confusion, Matthias had carried his stepson out to join the others.

At least they didn't have much time to worry. Emily could not help staring as they huddled together in the clearing between the bonfires. Dov stumbled into the circle to join them, as quiet as someone at a funeral. And that's what it felt like: a funeral for Kibbutz Yad Shalom, if not for its people.

Emily prayed quietly, and it seemed to calm the butterflies in her stomach. *If we're going to die, Lord,* she prayed, *help us to . . .*

To what? Her mind went blank, perhaps because she really did not know what to ask of God. She felt Henrik's mother, Ruth, take her hand as they walked to the fires.

Only Matthias dared speak. " 'If the earthly tent we live in is destroyed,' " he whispered, " 'we have a building from God, an eternal house in heaven, not built by human hands.' "

A building from God! Emily wondered if such a Scripture had been written especially for this occasion. Just then she wouldn't have minded seeing God's building. Anything but the nightmare they now faced: the ruined buildings, the fires, the laughing soldiers . . .

"Hurry!" grunted a soldier from behind her. She knew the Arabic word, and there was no mistaking the blunt jab of the rifle in her back. Dov narrowed his eyes and plodded on beside her. She knew he had heard this kind of thing before, perhaps made this kind of walk.

"Come!" cried the Egyptian commander, waving his hand in the air. One would have guessed he was inviting them to a picnic, rather than ... whatever he had planned. "I am Commander Abdullah al Moussa. Everyone come closer!"

The man could not have been older than her own father, and he spoke English with an accent heavier than a bomb dropping into the night air. Still, with some extra effort, Emily could understand him. She squinted and joined the others around the cheerless bonfire.

"This is our home." With Dov's help, Matthias set Henrik on the ground as gently as he could. "You have no right—"

Emily flinched, waiting for what would come next. But the protest was cut short when the commander fired a volley of gunshots over their heads.

"On the contrary." Commander al Moussa's rifle smoked and his eyes blazed with anger as the growing fire sparkled and reflected there. "You are the ones who have no rights, moving here, stealing Arab lands. Who gave you this place? The British?" He spat on the ground at their feet, narrowly missing where Henrik sat.

"As a matter of fact, we bought it from our Arab neighbors for a fair price." Matthias would not back down. "You could ask them yourself. We have always been good friends, until lately."

But the commander was not listening.

"I tell you this." His voice trembled as it grew louder. "We will liberate Palestine in three days, just as we have now liberated this place. By Allah, I promise that my men and I will march into Tel Aviv! And on the way, we will level every Jewish kibbutz. *Allah akhbar!*"

His men took up the cheer, waving their guns and raising their voices to the star-filled heavens. *"Allah akhbar!"* Over and over again. *"God is great!"*

Whose god? Emily closed her eyes and shivered at the sound— despite the fire's heat that now cooked her arms from two sides.

Whose God led this army into battle? And perhaps other armies from Syria and Lebanon and Iraq already camped on the borders of Jerusalem. That gave her all the more reason to deliver their emergency load of food—if it hadn't yet been discovered.

But she couldn't escape, let alone make it to the hiding place in the bushes only a few hundred yards away. She knelt in the dust, as crippled as Henrik. How could she ever return to Aunt Rachel, Uncle Anthony, and the girls at Saint Andrew's?

"What do you want with us?" Matthias braved yet another question. "Why are you destroying our home?"

Again Matthias made sure he used the word that seemed to anger the commander most. *Our* home. But this time the Egyptian didn't seem to notice.

"You will leave now," he told them. "I find no sport in killing unarmed farmers and peace fools. I fight with soldiers against soldiers. Not women and children . . . and cripples. When this is all over, you will understand our sense of honor."

Emily saw no honor in any of this, and she might have said so. But then Commander al Moussa motioned for one of his men to pump a bucket of water from the well.

"We stopped only for the water here," he explained. "My friend Fawzi says it is the best in the entire Gaza region. Isn't that right, Fawzi?"

Fawzi? There was no mistaking the Arab sound of *that* name.

Levin stepped up, looking rather pleased with himself. This was *Fawzi*? He dusted his hands off, bowed, and smiled.

"Absolutely, sir."

Commander al Moussa smiled as he dipped a tin cup into the bucket of water and held it out.

"Then you don't mind if we give our Jewish dogs—forgive me, I mean *guests,* a drink before they have to leave? It's the least we can do to reassure them of our hospitality, as well as to assure their comfort before their long journey north."

Emily could tell something was going on underneath the sugar-sweet cloud of the commander's words, something hard and cold. But she had no idea what.

"Of course." Levin took the cup and was about to hand it to Matthias when Dov stepped up.

"Here, I'll get it for you," he volunteered.

For a moment Emily saw Levin's eyes widen as they stared at each other. The cup trembled and sloshed in a minor tug-of-war until Levin shrugged his shoulders and released it to Dov.

"Be my guest," said Levin with a slight nod of his head.

"I once read a book of Jewish history," said Commander al Moussa. "You must know of Masada. There, all the Jews on the mountain fortress killed themselves before the Romans could conquer them. But I don't think the Jews of today are so brave, eh?"

Dov didn't take his eyes from Levin as he downed the cup of water in one swift gulp.

"I've never heard of Masada," he said, licking his lips.

Emily had, and she knew exactly what the commander was saying. For the next few minutes all they could hear was the crackling and popping of the fires as Dov refilled the cup and passed it around. Did he know something they didn't? Surely he wouldn't drink water that had been . . . well, *could it* have been poisoned? She didn't know until Dov turned to her with the bucket.

"Here, Emily. You should fill up a canteen before we leave. Go ahead, drink some." She could trust him. Emily took a long, cool drink herself, then finally held out the cup to Levin.

"How about you, Mr. Levin?" she asked. "Would you care for a—"

But Levin had already turned away. At the same time, Commander al Moussa's men began drawing water for the first of a long line of five-gallon metal jerry cans.

"Remove these people at once!" The commander switched

back to Arabic. "No time to waste! And get someone to help Fawzi with the water."

If he hadn't been so bone tired early the next morning, Dov would have skipped out of the Yad Shalom gates. But he hadn't slept at all, not on the cold dirt between the burned buildings. The smoldering ashes did nothing to warm him. He guessed no one else had slept, either, before the soldiers roused them in the pre-dawn gray.

"Do you really think they're going to let us go?" whispered Emily. She pulled a shawl around her shoulders to fight off an early chill.

Dov shrugged his shoulders and looked around. A few soldiers stood guard, but he really didn't want to see what the ruins of the kibbutz would look like by the light of day.

"Well, I'll tell you something." She lowered her voice. "If they do let us go, I'm going straight back around to see if the donkeys are still there."

"After all this?" Dov wondered where she found the energy to even think about it. "You think the food would still be there in the bushes, waiting for us—I mean, for you?"

"Who knows?" Emily held out her hands. "Either way, God is in control."

"So you're still thinking about bringing supplies to Jerusalem. . . ."

"And you're still thinking about finding your mother, aren't you? About getting to Tel Aviv and finding a way out to Cyprus."

He frowned but didn't answer.

"Aren't you?" she pressed him.

"Yes. I can't forget that sort of thing."

"I know that, Dov. So why would you think I would just

forget about what *I* still have to do?"

"You're right. You wouldn't." Dov had learned that Emily was almost as stubborn as he was. "But the question is, you think they'll let us go?"

"Moses might have asked the same question once."

Dov liked Moses' story. He just wished he knew the ending to this story, too.

DEATH MARCH

Within half an hour Dov and the others had been rousted up and forced to march single file out the front gate at bayonet point. No ceremonies, no good-byes. Just get out and don't come back.

Dov doubted the commander had even risen for his morning coffee. David Levin, on the other hand, seemed to have taken charge of the entire exodus. Dov had no idea why. Was he afraid they would become sick in front of the Egyptians?

"Come on, people!" Levin herded the last of them out the gate, waving his hand impatiently. "Hurry, before the commander changes his mind." He looked back over his shoulder at the dark tent where the commander had taken up residence.

Dov's thoughts returned to the story of Moses and the Exodus. Would anyone follow in a chariot? He didn't want to wait around to find out.

But it did seem that in this matter, Commander al Moussa was a man of his word. He had destroyed their kibbutz but let them go. And once they all cleared the gates, they would have only about thirty miles to Tel Aviv. Dov would be one step closer to a reunion with his mother. Wasn't that what he had wanted in the first place? Still, he now dragged his feet, even last in line. Poor

Julian dragged along just ahead of him, a bit more slowly than usual. The old dog had to be tired of traveling. More than once he looked back at Dov with sad eyes.

"What about everyone else?" asked Henrik. Riding in a wheelbarrow couldn't be comfortable, especially not with the splints on his legs and the bandages around his chest. Every bump had to hurt. But he almost made it look fun as the young men of the kibbutz took turns pushing him. "Is everyone going to Tel Aviv?"

Most nodded their heads yes. A few had friends in Kibbutz Ma'barot, with whom they thought they might stay. Others said they would try Kibbutz Gan Shmuel. No one dared mention Commander al Moussa's promise to level every kibbutz in his path.

Maybe he won't make it very far, Dov thought. *Maybe his soldiers will get homesick. Or just sick.*

At least that's what Levin hoped—of that Dov was certain. When Levin escorted them through the gate, the half dozen armed soldiers who guarded their flanks seemed happy enough to about-face and leave them alone. What more of a danger could these Jews be? The smell of smoke clung to their clothes. The dust of soldiers caked their hair. They certainly didn't look like any kind of threat.

"Too early to get up, eh?" Levin grinned and patted the last guard on the shoulder. He added something about going back to bed after chasing the Jews into the sea.

The soldier laughed and closed the gate behind them. Now they could officially call themselves *war refugees.*

"We meet back here at Yad Shalom as soon as the fighting lets up," Matthias announced a few minutes later. He didn't seem to care that Levin heard. "Agreed?"

"Here?" asked an older woman. She glanced nervously back at their escort, still dressed in his Arab robes. "What's left for us here now?"

"The land." Matthias wouldn't give up. "Don't you see? We

bought Yad Shalom from the Arabs, but God gave this land to us."

The woman didn't argue; they were only steps from their home, and everyone had lapsed into an exhausted silence. Dov tried not to wonder if perhaps she was right. What would anyone go back to now? Even Henrik's mother cried, her tears making tracks down dusty cheeks.

"Don't look back, dear." Matthias kept his arm around his wife as they walked. The road stretched ahead through rolling coastal hills, north toward Tel Aviv. Dov thought with a twinge of guilt that he might be the only one in the group who was glad to get away. But still he lagged behind, until Levin grabbed his arm.

"What was that stunt back at the well?" hissed the man.

Dov knew exactly what he was asking.

"What do you care?"

He stroked his beard. "Maybe I don't. It's just that I've never seen such a monumentally stupid move in my life. Especially after I warned you."

If he only knew. Dov couldn't think of a way to explain that the well was safe. He wasn't even sure he wanted to. Levin would find out in time.

"Warned you about what?" Emily had slipped back to see what was happening. "What is he talking about, Dov?"

Dov couldn't let his secret go. He shook his head.

"Well." Levin looked grim. "I'll leave you here, so good luck to you . . . for the rest of what could be a very short life."

David Levin wasn't through. "You may not be very smart—but at least you're loyal. I'll give you that."

"You needn't patronize him," snapped Emily. "What do you know about loyalty? You're for sale to the highest bidder."

For a moment Levin froze at the attack before shrugging it off. Dov thought he saw a trace of sadness in David Levin's eyes. Regret, maybe? Had he done things he wished he hadn't?

Finally Levin took a deep breath. "Whatever you say. For what it's worth, I *am* sorry it had to turn out this way. Shalom."

Dov and Emily watched as David Levin returned the way they had come, his shoulders slumped. And almost without meaning to, Dov prayed silently for the man.

"That's it, then." Emily turned to Dov, her hand out and jaw set. "And it's good-bye again."

But Dov did not take her hand. He looked at the disappearing line of kibbutzniks, glad that Julian was with Henrik for now. In the east, behind Emily, Dov thought he saw the first hints of dawn.

"Are you all right?" she asked.

"Sure, I'm all right." Dov straightened up and squared his shoulders. "Why do you ask?"

"No reason." She shook her head and lowered her hand. "You've just seemed . . . I don't know . . . *different* the last day or two."

But Dov wasn't about to spill everything to Emily, not just yet. For a moment he wondered if he could put into words what had happened, then sighed.

"I don't know if I can explain it," he told her at last. "Maybe later. But we'd better get moving if we're going to find those silly donkeys before the sun comes up."

Incredibly, the animals were still tied up where Henrik and Emily had left them Friday night, still contentedly chewing the once-thick grass around the overgrown thicket of trees where they'd been hidden. How the soldiers had not discovered their secret, Emily had no idea.

"But how are we going to load them again," whispered Dov, "without making too much noise?"

How, indeed? Emily wasn't certain of that, either. But she was sure they would need some kind of miracle to make it out of there without being seen—even *without* a load.

"One thing at a time, I guess." Dov began by loading baskets of grain and honey. Next came the onions and potatoes, which also still looked pretty good. But this process was taking far too long.

"Hurry!" Emily urged. Shadows were starting to lighten even in the dark, cool glade. They couldn't afford to wait there a full day.

Perhaps the leeks and cucumbers could. The cheese, however, had begun to turn a little green around the edges. Not that it mattered much to hungry children. And the eggs, still packed in sawdust, well, she didn't want to think about whether they would still be fine.

Ten minutes later, Emily crawled on her hands and knees to the edge of the bushes and peeked out at the kibbutz. What she saw made her gasp.

"It's Levin!" she whispered to Dov, who looked for himself. David Levin came right up next to the outer security fence with two young guards, walking with a searchlight. She was sure it was him from the sound of his voice.

"Doesn't matter," Dov told her. "We have to go now or we'll never get out of here."

"But it's not that dark anymore," Emily said. Dov had to know they were in a fix. "They'll see us."

Besides Levin and his friends by the fence, the guard in the tower would probably spot them once they got in the clear. Emily looked at Dov, her question unspoken.

"I say we go for it," he answered. "I think we'll make it fine."

Perhaps they would, if they hurried. But she never saw the twig that broke under her knee, though anyone could plainly hear the rifle shot of its snap.

Oh no! Emily froze but could not help looking to see if . . .

Levin saw her. He had to, the way his dark eyes locked on

hers. She slowly counted to three, waiting for the soldiers she was sure would come.

Wouldn't they?

Dov tugged on her ankle to pull her back to the safety of the bushes, but still she stared as Levin steered his companions away from the fence. Finally she backed away and returned to the animals.

"Come on!" Dov whispered and tossed one of the halter ropes to her. There was no time to talk, no time to do anything but run. Dov knew it as well as she did.

For the first few yards they were still in the shadow of the olive trees, the same ones that blocked their view of the watchtower.

"Keep praying," Dov told her. *He* was telling her to pray? My, did he have some explaining to do when they got out of this mess. The thought crossed her mind that if they did escape, she might find herself on the trail with someone who really wasn't Dov Zalinski.

But there was no time to think about that now. Emily *did* pray, though, for a few more minutes of darkness, for blindness to overtake the guards' eyes and deafness to stop their ears. She prayed, too, for the quickest path to freedom and that neither of them would stumble on the rocky path that led up a hill, away from the remains of Kibbutz Yad Shalom.

"Oh, do hurry," she whispered to her donkey. Emily hustled along behind her animal and just ahead of Dov's. She dared not slap the animal's backside for fear of making a noise, though their footfalls seemed loud enough to attract the attention of anyone within miles.

Step by step, they continued up the hill as fast as they dared. Still they heard nothing behind them, despite their latest encounter with David Levin. Or perhaps *because* of it. Could he actually be protecting them?

They continued climbing. A hundred feet, seventy-five,

fifty . . . Another twenty-five feet and they'd be over the first ridge, hopefully well out of sight.

It might as well have been twenty-five miles. Because just as Emily led her animal over the ridge and started to let out her breath, they heard a shout from below.

"You! Stop!"

Dov scrambled over the ridge just ahead of a volley of shots. Two skittered off boulders only feet away, sending explosions of wicked rock shards into their faces. Emily shrieked as splinters showered her cheek and neck.

Lizzi the donkey must have felt them, too, despite her thick hide. She brayed and bucked, nearly sending her load crashing down the hillside with Lizzi still attached.

"Whoa!" Dov tried to ignore the pain as he doubled the halter around his fist and held on with all his strength. The rope dug into his flesh, but still he held on.

Emily's animal caught the panic, as well, and began to buck. "Hold on!" Emily leaned into her load and hugged Laslo around the neck. If her donkey tumbled back down the hill, she would, too.

Dov wished for just one more hand to help her, but it was all he could do to keep his own animal from breaking loose.

At least the shooting had stopped—for the moment. And once they finally calmed the donkeys, Dov crawled up to the boulder and the hump in the hillside that now blocked their view of the kibbutz. It had been nearly dark when they started out, but now the sun already threatened to cast shadows behind them. Soon that sun would light the way for the three soldiers climbing the hill toward them as if it sloped down instead of up.

"Here they come." Emily groaned. "We're never going to get away."

"Yes, we are," insisted Dov.

Or at least she is.

Dov hoped that maybe the soldiers had not yet seen both of them. Maybe if they separated he could draw their attention away so that at least Emily could escape. But Emily wouldn't go along with that.

"Absolutely not," she told him.

"Don't be so stubborn." He glanced back down the hill. "We have five minutes at most before those soldiers are standing up here with us. Do you have any better ideas?"

Emily's mouth moved but nothing came out.

For once. Dov couldn't help grinning.

"I'll take Lizzi north, sideways, across the hills," he told her.

Emily nodded lamely. "What if they start shooting again?"

"If they do, I'll just hold up my hands and act dumb. Comes naturally."

"Oh, stop it."

"I'm not kidding. I'll tell them I found this animal, that they can have all the food, and that I need to get back to the group. Meanwhile, you get back to Jerusalem as fast as you can. Don't stop if you can help it."

Emily didn't smile. "I'm really sorry to leave you like this."

"Me too." Dov dusted himself off. "I didn't want you to cross the mountains alone. But you'll be fine."

She nodded as he dug into his backpack, then held out a small handful of slightly bent photographs.

"The ones you took on the ship?"

"Please take them."

She paused only a moment.

"Thank you, Dov."

"I'll see you again soon."

He turned to go, taking the halter in his hand. But there was more he wanted to tell her.

"Emily?"

Now had to be the worst time and place to say something like this. But if not now, when?

"Remember that you said I seemed different?"

"You do."

He took a deep breath. "I . . . I believe now."

She gave a puzzled shake of her head, as if she didn't quite follow.

"You believe what?"

"I believe like you and Henrik. In the Messiah. Yeshua."

Emily's face lit up, but it wasn't because of the sunrise that had crested the hill and bathed them in its golden light. For a moment they both might have forgotten the approaching danger.

"I always knew you would someday, Dov Zalinski."

Another shot hit the boulders only a few yards away. They both ducked and their donkeys bucked.

Dov gripped the bridle. "Bad timing."

"Not at all. I think your timing is rather . . . perfect." Emily waited another moment before she turned away, leaving Dov to travel his own way.

TEL AVIV

19

October 22, 1948

"Hey, not so fast!" Henrik laughed as they rolled around a corner of the living room on two wheels of his wheelchair.

Julian woofed at them from his spot on a small oval rug near the front door but didn't get up. Lately he hadn't been getting up much at all.

Dov grinned but didn't slow down as they rocketed across the tile floor.

"Whoa!" Good thing Matthias was quick on his feet. He skipped in through the front door and safely out of the way.

Dov wasn't nearly as quick.

"Sorry." He grabbed the back handle of the wheelchair and pulled himself off the floor. At least he hadn't dumped Henrik, which he'd already done once before.

"Looks as if you boys need to go for a run on the beach." Matthias stood with his arms crossed, but the grin on his face told Dov they weren't in trouble.

"Well, we're still working on beach wheels for my chair."

Dov had to smile. Five months in a wheelchair, and Henrik was still joking as much as ever. It didn't seem to matter to him that he might have to stay in that thing forever.

"So tell us the news." Henrik nodded at the piece of paper wadded in his stepfather's hand.

"I'll read it to you. To everybody! Ruth?" Matthias looked around the modest beach house they had rented for the past several months.

Henrik's mother peeked around the entry doorway. She nearly dropped her basket of laundry when she saw Matthias.

"I *thought* I heard a commotion up here in the front room. Matthias Karlsson, what are you doing home so early?"

"Listen to this." He was obviously enjoying the moment for all it was worth. With a flourish he unfolded the paper, but not before carefully removing a pair of spectacles from the hard case in his pocket.

"Here." Henrik rolled himself closer to Matthias and tried to snatch the paper away. "By the time you read that thing, I'm going to be an old man."

Matthias grinned at the teasing and backed up before beginning to read.

"The government has announced that as of today, Friday, October 22, an indefinite cease-fire exists between the State of Israel and all armed invading forces. All armed hostilities—"

"Woo-hoo!" Henrik interrupted with a loud whoop. "Does that mean the war is over?"

Matthias shook his head. "A cease-fire. The war's not over. But the shooting stops . . . for now."

"What does that mean?" Dov asked.

"That means we're going back to Yad Shalom!" Matthias linked arms with his wife and did a jig right in the middle of the living room.

Dov smiled and turned to look at the bright blue Mediterranean. Wave tops glittered in the setting sun as they had nearly every afternoon since they'd come to Tel Aviv. But those beautiful waves had also kept him from his mother.

"I'm sorry you haven't seen her yet, Dov." Henrik came up behind him, lightly bumping Dov's calves with the wheelchair leg rests. "But you know if anybody can help, it's Matthias."

"I know."

"I mean, he helped return Emily to her father, so . . ."

"He's done everything he can for me." Dov managed half a smile. He *did* appreciate the effort, but what now? "At least you've had somebody to push you around for the past few months."

"That's right. My own personal slave!"

It felt good to laugh. Even so far from his mother, Dov knew he had plenty to celebrate. Everything had changed since Henrik saved his life during the attack. And he knew his life had been saved in another way, a better way.

Even so . . . Dov bit his lip and watched the waves for another moment before turning back to the celebration.

"What does that second page say?" Henrik wheeled himself closer to where Matthias stood.

Matthias shook his head, leaned against the kitchen wall, and replaced the glasses in his pocket. He exchanged a quick glance with his wife.

"Oh, come on." Henrik made another grab. But Matthias was clearly done.

"You'll find out soon enough." And with that Matthias turned on his heel and disappeared into the other room.

Emily stood in front of the mirror, once more adjusting the buttons on her dress and the beret in her hair.

What if Daddy changes his mind at the last minute? she fretted. *What if . . .*

But no. Everything was ready. After weeks of her pleading, he'd finally agreed. And they'd be flying, no less. All the way back across the Mediterranean!

Emily twirled in place in front of the mirror, like the miniature ballerina on her jewelry box. *Only far clumsier,* she thought.

A soft knock on her bedroom door brought her back to reality.

"Ready, Emily?" asked her mother. Her voice sounded clear, without a trace of the tears she'd shed the night before. That was Mother for you. Stiff upper lip. Only a few months earlier she'd vowed that Emily would never again leave England. And now...

"Coming!" Emily gave one last glance around her room, at the frilly bed that really wasn't her style, at the refugee ship photos that Dov had given her, and at the other photo of Julian sitting in their kitchen, back home in Jerusalem.

"Coming!" she repeated, heading for the door.

RETURN TO
DESTRUCTION

20

A month after the cease-fire was announced, Dov stood staring at the place he had escaped with Emily Parkinson and the donkeys. Had only six months passed since then? It seemed much longer—or shorter, he couldn't decide which. Weeks tumbled and twisted in his memory.

In any case, the war had dragged on far too long. They had read about it every day in the papers, sometimes hearing the explosions in the distance. Dov had almost gotten used to the sound of destruction. He'd also received a couple of letters from Emily in England. She was doing fine but missed Jerusalem, missed Julian, missed everything except the war.

Getting used to waiting was the hardest part. At first Dov had thought he could just hop on a boat to Cyprus to go see his mother. But of course it wasn't that simple—nothing was simple anymore.

And now he faced another scene from a nightmare: Everything at Yad Shalom had been destroyed. Everything. The kibbutz was in far worse condition than he remembered.

"I can't believe it. . . ." he muttered, staring at the wreckage. The sound of singing coming from the kibbutz made him jump as a truck dropped off two more families. Some dragged battered suitcases, others arrived with their arms full of overflowing cardboard boxes. Obviously they'd all heard it was safe to return to the kibbutz. But Dov wasn't sure they saw the same thing he did.

"What's wrong with these people?" Dov asked. "Can't they see what a horrible mess this is?"

Anyone would have been blind not to notice. None of the dozen or so buildings remained; all had been leveled, except for half of one concrete wall of the old dining hall. Everyone gathered there. The ditches they had dug had been filled with disgusting piles of barbed wire and garbage, twisted metal, chunks of concrete. The grape vineyard had been pulled up and burned, and all the grass had been trampled. The only thing that seemed to remain untouched was the well.

"Yes, they can see." Matthias leveled his gaze at Dov. "You never saw what this place looked like when we arrived the first time."

"Worse than this?"

"Well, maybe not worse." He shrugged his shoulders. "But we fixed this place up once. We'll do it again, Lord willing. Right, Henrik?"

Henrik was stuck in a sand puddle; Dov went over to push him free.

"Now we're going to have to add ramps for your wheelchair," Matthias smiled.

"A wheelchair ramp is one thing," said Dov. "Rebuilding everything is another."

"Details, details." Matthias bent to pick up a spent bullet cartridge and tossed it toward a growing pile. Dov also bent to work, clearing the once-grassy courtyard area in front of the dining hall.

"Are we going to put up our tents soon?" Dov pointed at the pile of canvas and stakes they'd brought along. The sun would be setting behind the western dunes in a couple of hours.

But Matthias only smiled and shook his head. "Time enough for all that."

A man had showed up with his accordion, and a minute later they had formed a circle dance, a *hora* dance of celebration. Once more the land was theirs, as Matthias reminded them all. Dov and Henrik watched, off to the side, as the sun sank lower and the dance grew. Once or twice Henrik's mother and Matthias waved for them to join them. Dov stood behind Henrik's chair, pretending he was needed.

"Henrik," he asked quietly. "Do you ever ask why?"

"Why what?"

Dov thought of dropping the subject, but . . .

"Why this." He kicked at the wheelchair.

"Oh, *that* why." Henrik shrugged and paused for a minute before answering. "Once. Just after that doctor in Tel Aviv told me . . . you know."

That he will probably never walk again.

Dov nodded. "I remember that day."

"I didn't get an answer, in case you were wondering. I guess I'm going to have to wait awhile to dance again."

They stood in silence a few minutes; then, as the music grew louder and louder, Dov grabbed the handle and leaned on it, sending Henrik's feet into the air.

"Whoa! What are you doing?" Henrik clearly wasn't sure what to make of Dov's latest move.

"We're going to dance, my friend. I mean, *you* are."

"Wha—?"

"Don't argue." Before anyone could change his mind, Dov wheeled Henrik around to the back of the circle.

"Coming through!"

The dancers smiled and opened up the line. They seemed to get the idea sooner than Henrik.

"Put out your hands!" Dov ordered.

Henrik did, grabbing hold from each side. And as they sang and danced, Dov kept the wheelchair in motion, right and left, straight in, back out, round and round. They all laughed until they nearly cried, laughed until they saw a large gray sedan tearing down the road toward them, kicking up a cyclone of dust. The accordion faltered and stopped as they all stopped to stare.

"Well, some of us have done a little better than the rest of us poor workers," muttered a man standing beside Dov. He had meant it as a joke, and three or four people laughed nervously. The sedan pulled up and stopped, but stare as he might, Dov could not see through the car windows.

Dov gaped as the front door opened and Major Alan Parkinson stepped outside. Well, at least it looked like the major. He was out of uniform, wearing a rumpled blue suit that appeared to have been traveled in for a day or two.

The major reached for the back door handle, but that door had already popped open. Dov nearly swallowed his tongue when Emily Parkinson emerged.

"Better watch for bugs flying into your mouth." Henrik grinned up at him, and Dov snapped his jaw shut. "Are you going to roll me over there, or are you just going to keep staring?"

Dov did his best to roll Henrik through a sandy patch to the middle of a welcoming committee that included Henrik's mother and Matthias.

"I'm so pleased you could make it." Matthias held out his hand in greeting. "I wasn't quite sure our cable arrived."

"It did." Major Parkinson returned the smile. "As you know, my Emily can be rather, er . . . persuasive. And your reputation, Mr. Karlsson, goes before you. I'm glad to finally make your acquaintance."

Emily dropped to her knees and took Henrik's hands. "I'm so happy to see you again, Henrik. You don't know how much this invitation means to me."

Invitation? Dov was confused.

"We didn't want you to be disappointed if they couldn't make it for some reason," explained Matthias. "But did she . . ."

He looked first at Major Parkinson, then at Emily.

"Go on, Emily." The major patted her shoulder. "Let's not keep her waiting in the car."

Emily hurried around to the other side of the Plymouth, opened the door, and leaned inside. A moment later she emerged, holding the hand of a frail-looking but very beautiful woman, dark-haired and dark-eyed like Dov. The woman's paper-thin legs looked as if they might fold at any moment, but as she gamely stepped toward the group, her eyes locked on Dov's.

Dov saw and heard nothing else—not the singing in the background nor the crackling of the warm fire they had built. Not even Emily saying, "Everyone, I'd like you to meet a good friend of mine, Leah Zalinski. This is Dov's mother."

Imma!

It took some time for the tears to end. But of course these were the good kind, tears of joy.

"I left you in tears the last time I saw you," recalled Imma. Even in the dusk, Dov saw the far-off look in her eyes as she stared across the dunes to the west. She had not let go of his hand since she had arrived an hour earlier.

Someone had brought a packing crate for her to sit on, which they had placed on the far side of Major Parkinson's borrowed car. And so they sat together, Dov on the ground, his mother on the box, enjoying the early evening breeze coming in from the ocean, laced with a friendly hint of the Mediterranean and unseasonably warm for November. They talked quietly, remembering the sweet Before, comparing a few painful details from the bitter During, and now daring to mention what could happen in the After. Without thinking of what she might say, he told her of his Messiah, then stopped abruptly and bit his tongue.

Will she think I betrayed her? he asked himself.

But Imma's grip only tightened, and with her free hand she gently combed the hair off of his forehead.

"You sound just like your friend Emily." Her voice sounded as warm as the breeze he felt.

Dov could see his mother's face clearly, even in the dark—the same face that had last seen him standing alone on the orphanage steps in Warsaw, before the war. And he remembered her promise to come back for him.

"Do you remember you told me we would go to Jerusalem together?" he asked.

"Every day I remembered that promise, Little Bear."

"You said we could celebrate my *bar mitzvah* at the *Kotel,* the Wall."

"Perhaps we still can. But look at you! You've turned into a man, even without me."

She tightened her grip, and Dov's eyes once more filled with tears as she began to hum the song she had begun so many years ago. Her soft, sweet voice whispered out the musical Hebrew words.

"Yevarechecha ha'Shem mi'Zion . . . Shalom al Israel."

Dov knew the words to the old folk song as surely as if they had been written on his heart.

The God of Zion shall bless you, and you shall see the goodness of Jerusalem. You shall see children and grandchildren. And peace shall be on Israel.

Peace? Dov smiled as he flicked away another empty bullet shell. Yet for the first time in his life, he was sure in his heart the words were true.

NATAN'S BAR MITZVAH

August 3, 1967

Emily Zalinski held her husband's hand tightly as they squeezed through the crowds at the Old City's Dung Gate and headed up the steps. How the Old City had changed in nineteen years! But nowhere more so than the Kotel, the most special place for every beating Jewish heart. She could only guess what was going through Dov's mind just then, though she could feel his pulse quicken as they drew closer.

"Wow," Nate repeated, his eyes wide. Before today their son had never stepped inside the Old City walls. He was only thirteen, the age all good Jewish boys looked forward to their bar mitzvah ceremony.

"You really lived here, Dad?" By the way Nate's eyes darted from side to side, he was noticing everything. He was just like his father that way. According to Dov, he was also a lot like his uncle Natan, for whom he was named.

Dov smiled as his eyes took on that faraway, remembering look. "Well," he answered, "it was a long time ago. Before the Jordanians captured the Old City."

Of course Nate had heard all the stories. But still he shook his head, as if trying to make sense of the tangled history of their country, their City of Peace, their Jerusalem no longer divided. How had a foreign army occupied the ancient heart of the city for so long? And why had it taken another war to liberate this place? Emily prayed Nate might grow old before the next war—whenever that might be.

"Now listen, you two," said Rachel, holding up a finger as they walked. Nate called her Aunt Rachel rather than his great-aunt, which wouldn't have suited her at all. She looked sternly at Dov. "No war talk when Anthony catches up with us."

"*If* he catches up." Dov looked at his watch. "I told him we wanted to start by noon, before the rabbis show up and we're—"

"Before we're chased off, right, Dad?" Nate grinned and took the large Bible from his father's hands. "If anybody bothers us, I'll just tell them my dad is Dov Zalinski, the famous war hero. Like you said, you're as Jewish as anyone else here."

Emily laughed. Their oldest son had learned well. It was Nate who insisted on holding his bar mitzvah at the Wall, when they could have done it back in their small house church, where no one would have noticed them. But no, Nate would read the Scripture here, in the middle of the crowds and all the people praying. And dogs barking.

"What's that?" Emily turned to see the source of the noise—a medium-sized, mixed-breed dog dragging a leash, looking much like its grandfather, the Great Dane she had once owned.

"Oh no." Dov moaned as they waited for the dog and a winded Uncle Anthony to catch up.

"I'm ... terribly ... sorry." Anthony snubbed the end of the leash and leaned on Dov's shoulder to catch his breath. "I had Juliette tied up outside the gate, but—"

"That dog!" interrupted Emily.

"She wanted to be here with everyone." Nate bent down and scratched Juliette's ears, leading her away to a pile of rubble on the far side of the Kotel square, far enough away to not attract any more attention than they already had. After tying her to the trunk of a rather short olive tree, he trotted back to the small group: Dov and Emily, Uncle Anthony and Aunt Rachel, and Batya and Chava—who had remained friends all these years and who now attended the small church meeting in their Talbiya neighborhood apartment. Emily's parents had not been able to make it, but they had sent a lovely bouquet of lilies. Old Mrs. Abernathy from Saint Andrew's had wanted to come, too, but her arthritis had flared up. And Dov's mother . . .

Thank you, Lord, Emily prayed as the men approached the wall. Over the years she had come to love her dear mother-in-law. *Thank you that she lived long enough to find you, as well.*

And then Nate began to read in the clear, strong voice that reminded Emily he was half boy, half man. A few other worshipers stopped to listen as Nate continued from the book of Isaiah.

"The spirit of the Lord God is on me, because the Lord has anointed me to bring good tidings to the afflicted; he has sent me to bind up the brokenhearted, to proclaim liberty to the captives, and the opening of the prison to those who are bound; to proclaim the year of the Lord's favor and the day of vengeance of our God; to comfort all who mourn; to grant to those who mourn in Zion . . ."

Emily caught her husband's eye, felt his quiet warmth as Nate kept reading.

"—to give them a garland instead of ashes, the oil of gladness instead of mourning, the mantle of praise instead of a faint spirit; that they may be called oaks of righteousness, the planting of the Lord, that he may be glorified."

Now her own oak was standing before them, reading. Here. Who would have thought?

"They shall build up the ancient ruins, they shall raise up the former devastations; they shall repair the ruined cities, the devastations of many generations."

Thank you. For Emily, every breath in this city was a prayer. And by now everyone standing by the Kotel had hushed to listen to these words. Everyone except her son, who seemed not to notice and kept reading.

"For Zion's sake I will not keep silent," read Nate, "and for Jerusalem's sake I will not rest, until her vindication goes forth as brightness, and her salvation as a burning torch."

MORE THAN HISTORY

May 14 marks a special day for Jews all over the world. On that day in 1948, David Ben-Gurion read a proclamation of independence declaring a free Jewish State as he became its acting prime minister. Israel was born, or rather, reborn.

But that was only the beginning. The Jews in Palestine soon discovered it would be much harder to create a country than just *saying* they had one. They would have to *fight*, as well. Within hours of the proclamation, the armies of seven neighboring states had invaded—including forces from Egypt, Jordan, Syria, Iraq, Saudi Arabia, Yemen, and Lebanon.

True Betrayer is based on the actual invasion timeline, focusing on the advance of Egyptian forces north through Gaza on their way to Tel Aviv. They did not actually make it to Israel's number-two city, however, and eventually withdrew as the war of independence drew to a close in late 1948 and early 1949.

The secret trail over the mountains in our story is based on actual historical fact, as well, though I have shifted the timing of its discovery slightly. It was discovered by three Jewish soldiers in May 1948 as they moved east through the hills and ravines outside Jerusalem and finally arrived at a place called Kibbutz Hulda. A few days later, one hundred fifty more Jewish soldiers in jeeps traveled from Hulda toward Jerusalem. When they met with jeeps coming west three hours later, they knew they had found a way through the blockade of Jerusalem.

They called it the Burma Road, after a tough mountain pass in Asia carved out by Allied forces during World War II. As this road may have been just as treacherous to travel, its impact was mainly symbolic. Jeeps and donkeys could simply not carry enough food and supplies across the trail to make a difference in Jerusalem. Today, iron skeletons remain along portions of the road, reminders of the bloody battles fought in the hills around Jerusalem.

The character of David Levin is inspired by a real Israeli agent named Ezra Horin, who was sent with another agent to the coastal area of Gaza just as Egyptian troops were advancing. Their job was to learn all they could about the army and, if possible, sabotage the march north. However, both men were captured before they could carry out their mission, and afterward the Egyptian press reported that "Ezra Horin of Tel Aviv admitted that he brought a canteen full of typhus and dysentery germs with him to Gaza, intending to dump it into a well and poison the whole Egyptian Army."

The first war continued until a fragile peace took hold by early 1949. The first elections in the new state were held January 25, 1949, making Israel the only democratic country in the Middle East.

Even so, one major problem remained for the Israelis—the continued occupation of the Old City by Jordanian forces. These troops remained in place until May 1967, when they gave way during the Six-Day War that took place between June 5 and June 10 of that year.

Those are just a fraction of the historical and military facts about how modern-day Israel began. It's not hard to see how that history relates to what we hear and read in today's news reports. Peace is still rare and precious in that part of the world.

Yet even more interesting than the story of modern-day Israel is the story of God's people in this land—particularly those who have chosen to follow the Messiah Yeshua, or Jesus. For many years there was only a handful of Jewish people in Israel who claimed to follow Jesus. But since then God's Spirit has been moving, and today there are hundreds like Rachel and Dov. Hundreds who are part of a tree of faith that includes both Arabs and Jews, as well as millions more people from places all over the globe. Labels are ultimately lost in this family of faith. By following the Messiah, we all become the "children of the promise" written about in Romans chapter 9.

By choosing to follow Yeshua, these Jews are not, as some have said, converted to an alien religion of crusaders and invaders. Rather, they are complete in the faith of their fathers as they come to know the "author and perfecter of our faith" (Hebrews 12:2).

In that author rests the only hope for lasting peace in Israel, the only true hope for peace between Palestinian and Jew. The only ultimate hope for peace for all of us, wherever we might live.

FROM THE AUTHOR

 The adventures don't stop with the last page of this book! Here are several ideas for you to try:

1. *Discover other books.* I've put together a list of some of my favorite books, magazines, Web sites, music, and more on Israel. They'll help you get a better feel for the strange and wonderful land Dov and Emily came to. Be sure to show this section to your parents or teacher.

2. *Write to me.* I always enjoy hearing from readers, and I answer all my mail. How did you like the book? Did you have a question about anything that happened or about what the characters were thinking? What's next? My address is: Bethany House Publishers, 11400 Hampshire Avenue South, Bloomington, MN, 55438 USA.

3. *Go online.* Visit my Web site at *www.elmerbooks.org.* That's where you can learn more about my books, read a little about me, and find out the answers to many of your questions. Check out *www.bethanyhouse.com,* too, for more information on other good books.

Shalom!

Robert Elmer

WANT TO KNOW MORE?

The library, bookstands, and even the Internet are full of great resources for learning more about Israel and about the incredible events that happened there between 1946 and 1949. Here are a few ideas to get you started.

Picture Books on Israel

- *The Bible Lands Holyland Journey,* by Dr. Randall D. Smith. Published by Doko in Israel, this is one of the better picture books of Israel and the Holy Land I've found. You'll see pictures of many of the places Dov and Emily visit.

History

- *To the Promised Land* by Uri Dan (Doubleday, 1988). An excellent book full of historic photos, this was created to celebrate Israel's fortieth anniversary. Be sure to check out the chapter on the Burma Road, the trail across the mountains that helped to supply Jerusalem.
- *The Best of Zvi* by Zvi Kalisher. This man's story inspired many of the events in Dov Zalinski's life. In fact, I had a chance to interview him personally in his Jerusalem home. What a story—truth is even more exciting than fiction! The book is available through the Friends of Israel Gospel Ministry in New Jersey, P.O. Box 908, Bellmawr, NJ 08099.
- *The Creation of Israel* by Linda Jacobs Altman (Lucent Books World History Series, 1998). A good all-in-one history of how Israel was founded, this book has a useful timeline, index, and

pictures, too. A perfect resource for a student's research paper.

- *Child of the Warsaw Ghetto* by David Adler, illustrated by Karen Ritz (Holiday House, 1995). Some of the scenes in this picture book are sad and hard to look at, but it helps to know what people like Dov went through during the worst days of World War II.

Hebrew

- *Hebrew for Everyone,* published and distributed by Epistle. Here's a fun, kid-friendly approach to learning the language of the Old Testament—and today's Israel! The study guide is written by Jewish believers in Jesus and is designed for kids and beginners. You can learn the Lord's Prayer in Hebrew! I picked up my copy at the Garden Tomb in Jerusalem for twenty shekels. (A shekel is about twenty-five cents.) Contact Epistle at P.O. Box 2817, Petach Tikva, 49127, Israel.

Internet

- International Christian Embassy of Jerusalem (*www.icej.org.il*) is a good place to start for all kinds of links to travel and historic information on Jerusalem and Israel.
- The U.S. Holocaust Memorial Museum (*www.ushmm.org*) is the leading museum in North America for information on what happened to the Jewish people before, during, and after World War II.

Music

- *Hora—The Most Famous 25 Israeli Folk Songs.* Hear some of the songs mentioned in the book, like the song Dov's mom sang, "Yevarechecha." They're fun to listen to, and they'll help you sound out some of those unusual but beautiful Hebrew words!

Courage
Takes Center Stage

ADVENTURES DOWN UNDER

Escape to Murray River
Captive at Kangaroo Springs
Rescue at Boomerang Bend
Dingo Creek Challenge
Race to Wallaby Bay
Firestorm at Kookaburra Station
Koala Beach Outbreak
Panic at Emu Flat

With exciting plots that will take your breath away and interesting glimpses at one of the most fascinating far off places, Robert Elmer's series ADVENTURES DOWN UNDER spins the globe to deliver you to the rough-and-tumble outback of Australia in the 1860s.

YOUNG UNDERGROUND

A Way Through the Sea
Beyond the River
Into the Flames
Far From the Storm
Chasing the Wind
A Light in the Castle
Follow the Star
Touch the Sky

Through their hold-your-breath adventures with the Danish Underground, Peter and Elise will lead you into a time and place you'll never forget. The harbor city of Helsignor, occupied by Nazis, proves an ideal place for the young siblings to live out their faith as they make their own stand against the evil terrorizing Europe.

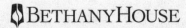
BETHANYHOUSE

11400 Hampshire Ave S. Minneapolis, MN 55438
(866) 241-6733 www.bethanyhouse.com
Source Code: BOBRE